Raised Among Giants

A Torlan Tarsen Adventure

Raised Among Giants

Russell V McFall

Ordained Path Books

Published by **Ordained Path Books**
For permissions or inquiries, contact:
ordainedpathbooks@gmail.com

Cover illustration and interior artwork generated by AI under direction of the author.

First Edition

ISBN (Paperback): 978-1-972724-00-2
ISBN (Hardcover):

Printed in the United States of America.

Version 1.02 -- March 2026

Dedication

For my children,
who first heard these stories long before they were written.
Your curiosity and imagination made these worlds possible.

Contents

Chapter 1 — The Journey to Hope 1
Chapter 2 — The Stranger in the Valley 11
Chapter 3 — Lyara's Garden 19
Chapter 4 — A Difficult Choice 27
Chapter 5 — The First Steps 34
Chapter 6 — The Light Beyond the Valley 40
Chapter 7 — The Young Varik 46
Chapter 8 — The Children of Valaryn 52
Chapter 9 — The Day of the Trial 58
Chapter 10 — The Night of the Storm 64
Chapter 11 — The Library of Valaryn 71
Interlude — The Search for *Horizon Dawn* 79
Chapter 12 — The Strength of the Body 84
Chapter 13 — The First Rescue 90
Chapter 14 — The Night Alone 97
Chapter 15 — The Name of Endurance 104
Chapter 16 — The Storm That Changed Valaryn 111
Chapter 17 — The Weight of Two Worlds 118
Chapter 18 — The Signal in the Sky 124
Chapter 19 — The Visitors from Earth 130
Chapter 20 — The Choice of Torlan 136
Epilogue — The Man from Cyrion 143
Author's Note 148
Appendix I — The People of Valaryn 150
Appendix II — Selected Words of the Cyrion Language 154
Appendix III — World Guide to Cyrion 158
Appendix IV — A Short Timeline of the *Horizon Dawn* 160
Appendix V — Ships of the Story 164
Appendix VI — A Map of the Valley of Valaryn 166
A Map of the Valley of Valaryn 167
About the Author 171
Also by Russell McFall 172

Chapter 1 — The Journey to Hope

The colony ship **Horizon Dawn** moved silently through the dark between the stars.

It was not a large vessel by the standards of interstellar travel, but every system aboard it had been built with a single purpose—to carry the first settlers to a world where humanity could begin again.

Thirty people lived within the vessel's curved hull.

They were engineers and farmers, builders and scientists. Some were young enough to see the colony grow from its first foundations. Others were older, chosen for their experience and wisdom.

Each of them had left something behind.

Cities. Families. Entire lives on distant worlds that had grown crowded and restless.

Ahead of them lay a planet discovered years earlier by long-range survey probes.

The settlers had given it a name long before any human eyes had seen it.

Hope.

Life Between the Stars

Months of travel had turned the routines of the ship into something almost peaceful.

In the residential ring, lights glowed softly along curved corridors where the settlers moved about their daily work. The air carried the faint scent of growing plants from the hydroponic bays.

Near the center of the vessel, a small communal hall served as the gathering place for meals and conversation. Earlier that evening laughter had filled the room as the settlers shared the end of another quiet day.

Some spoke about the structures they planned to build once they reached their destination.

Others debated the climate models that the survey probes had returned.

A few simply enjoyed the rare luxury of quiet.

Beyond the common hall, automated harvest arms moved gently through long rows of green plants. Tomatoes, leafy vegetables, and grains grew beneath artificial sunlight, tended by careful environmental controls.

Life aboard the **Horizon Dawn** had settled into a rhythm that felt almost ordinary.

Which was precisely what the settlers had hoped for.

The Observation Deck

From the forward observation deck the stars looked close enough to touch.

They shone through the curved viewing glass like scattered diamonds against the endless black.

For most of the passengers aboard the ship, the sight had long since become familiar. Months of travel had turned wonder into something closer to routine.

But tonight the observation deck was not empty.

William Arden stood near the window, one hand resting lightly against the rail as he studied the quiet field of stars.

Behind him the gentle hum of the ship's life-support systems filled the corridor with a steady, reassuring rhythm.

In his arms, his infant son slept peacefully.

The child's breathing was soft and steady, his tiny fingers curled around the edge of William's sleeve as though even in sleep he had decided not to let go.

William smiled faintly.

Elena

"Still awake?" a voice asked from the doorway.

William turned and saw Elena Arden stepping onto the observation deck.

The soft corridor lights caught the warmth in her tired expression. She had been working late again in the ship's biology lab, reviewing atmospheric and soil data gathered by the survey probes.

She moved quietly beside him and looked down at the sleeping child.

"He finally gave in," William said softly.

Elena brushed a finger lightly against the baby's hand.

Bill tightened his grip around William's sleeve.

She laughed quietly.

"He already thinks you're responsible for everything."

William looked back toward the stars beyond the glass.

"In a way," he said, "I suppose I am."

Elena followed his gaze.

Somewhere among those distant lights was the system they had spent nearly a year traveling toward.

A place no human had ever stood.

A place where thirty people aboard this ship hoped to build the beginning of a new life.

She leaned gently against his shoulder.

"Do you ever wonder what it will really look like?" she asked.

William nodded slowly.

"Every day."

He glanced down at the sleeping child in his arms.

"He'll grow up there," he said quietly.

"Under a sky no one has seen before."

For a moment the observation deck fell silent except for the steady hum of the ship.

Then somewhere deeper in the vessel, far behind the living ring, a warning light flickered briefly across a control panel.

No one on the observation deck noticed.

A Quiet Ship

Elena eventually returned to the biology lab to finish her work.

William remained at the observation window a while longer.

Across the ship, the evening routine continued as it had for months.

Lights dimmed in the residential compartments as settlers finished their work shifts. Environmental systems adjusted the temperature of the sleeping quarters.

In the hydroponic bay, automated harvest arms continued their careful trimming of the growing plants.

It was the calm, ordinary rhythm of a ship that had traveled safely through space for a very long time.

Then the lights flickered.

Just once.

William looked up.

The observation deck lights steadied again almost immediately.

For a moment he wondered if he had imagined it.

Ships were complex machines. Small fluctuations happened from time to time.

Still, something about the flicker lingered in his thoughts.

He gently laid Bill into the padded seat beside the observation window and tapped the console mounted along the wall.

The ship's system display appeared.

Everything looked normal.

Propulsion systems steady.

Life-support nominal.

Course vector unchanged.

William relaxed slightly and leaned back against the rail.

Behind the walls of the observation deck, the engines of the **Horizon Dawn** continued their quiet work—converting energy into the steady push that carried the vessel through interstellar space.

For several minutes nothing happened.

Then the ship shuddered.

It was subtle.

So slight that at first William thought it might simply be turbulence from the drive field adjusting its course.

But this time the lights flickered again.

And stayed dim.

The First Warning

A soft chime sounded from the console.

A line of text appeared across the display.

PROPULSION FIELD VARIANCE DETECTED

William frowned.

He tapped the screen again, pulling up the engineering readout.

One of the drive regulators showed a minor fluctuation.

Still within operational tolerance.

But unusual.

Before he could study it further, the ship's internal communication system activated.

"Engineering to command deck," a voice said calmly. "We're seeing a slight irregularity in the primary drive field. Nothing critical yet. We're investigating."

The voice belonged to **Chief Engineer Maren Holt**.

William recognized the steady tone immediately.

If Holt sounded calm, things were probably still under control.

He glanced at the sleeping child beside him.

Bill remained completely unaware that anything had changed.

Concern

Ten minutes passed.

Then twenty.

The lights dimmed again.

This time they did not recover fully.

Across the corridor outside the observation deck, footsteps moved quickly as crew members began heading toward their stations.

The communication system activated again.

This time the voice carried a different tone.

Still controlled.

But more serious.

"Attention all personnel," Holt said.

"Engineering is responding to an instability in the propulsion regulators. Please remain in your assigned areas until further notice."

William straightened.

A propulsion instability was not something settlers liked to hear.

He tapped the console again.

The drive regulator fluctuation had increased.

Still not dangerous.

But no longer minor.

The Escalation

A second warning tone sounded.

This one louder.

DRIVE FIELD CONTAINMENT SHIFT

The display flickered.

For the first time since the journey began, the ship's navigation system recalculated its trajectory.

William felt the faint vibration through the deck beneath his feet.

Somewhere deep within the hull, powerful systems were attempting to stabilize the engine field.

Then the communication system spoke again.

"Command to all crew," Holt said.

There was no attempt now to hide the seriousness of the situation.

"We are experiencing an uncontrolled drive cascade. Emergency containment procedures are in progress."

The words hung in the quiet room.

William felt his chest tighten.

Drive cascade.

That was not a small problem.

That was the kind of problem ships were built specifically to prevent.

The Realization

Another tremor passed through the ship.

This time strong enough to rattle the observation rail.

Bill stirred and began to wake.

William lifted him quickly into his arms.

Across the ship, emergency lighting shifted from white to amber.

The navigation display updated again.

William stared at the new trajectory.

His heart sank.

The ship was no longer following its original course.

The drive failure had pushed them off vector.

And directly toward an uncharted planetary body.

The Descent

The communication system activated once more.

"Attention all personnel," Holt's voice said.

"We have lost drive containment. The vessel is entering uncontrolled descent toward a nearby planetary body."

The words echoed through the corridors.

"Emergency landing procedures are in effect. Secure yourselves immediately."

William reached the residential compartment and secured Bill into a padded emergency seat.

The restraint system locked gently into place.

Bill stared up at him with wide, confused eyes.

William forced a reassuring smile.

"You're going to be fine," he whispered.

Then the ship began to shake.

Outside the hull the distant planet was growing rapidly larger.

Cloud systems stretched across its surface like enormous spirals.

Lightning flickered within towering storm formations.

The navigation display flashed red.

ATMOSPHERIC ENTRY IMMINENT

Impact

The first contact with the atmosphere came suddenly.

The ship lurched.

Outside the viewing ports, streaks of fire slid across the hull.

Air resistance roared around the vessel.

Internal stabilizers struggled to compensate.

"Shields holding," Holt's voice reported.

"For now."

Then came the sound no crew ever wanted to hear.

A long metallic groan.

The sound of a structure under stress.

The Valley

Below the falling ship, the planet **Cyrion** turned slowly beneath thick layers of cloud.

Between the storms lay a wide valley surrounded by towering stone formations.

Wind moved across the landscape in long sweeping currents.

High above, the burning shape of the **Horizon Dawn** tore through the sky.

Silence

The ground rushed upward.

The ship struck the valley floor with terrible force.

Metal screamed.

Sections of the hull tore apart as the vessel plowed through rock and soil.

The **Horizon Dawn** slid across the valley floor, carving a deep scar through the earth before finally coming to rest against a ridge of stone.

Then everything became still.

Alarms stopped.

Lights faded.

Smoke drifted slowly through broken corridors.

Outside the wreckage, the wind moved quietly across the valley.

Above the shattered hull, the twin moons of Cyrion rose slowly into the night sky.

The Only Survivor

Deep within the damaged structure, a small emergency cradle remained sealed.

Inside it, the infant slept.

Protected by systems designed for exactly this moment.

Hours later, far across the valley, a sensor in the town of **Valaryn** recorded the atmospheric disturbance.

And a scientist named **Dr. Arel Ziv** turned his eyes toward the distant horizon.

Chapter 2 — The Stranger in the Valley

Morning came slowly to the valley of **Valaryn**.

The first light of Cyrion's sun spread across the eastern ridges, touching the tall stone formations that guarded the valley like silent sentinels. For a time the upper cliffs glowed gold while the valley floor remained cool and blue beneath the fading shadows of night.

A thin layer of mist drifted across the fields where gardens and orchards surrounded the town. Dew gathered along the edges of stone pathways and clung to the wide leaves of the valley plants.

The air was still.

Then the birds began to sing.

Their voices echoed softly between the stone walls as the people of Valaryn began their morning routines.

Doors opened along the narrow paths that wound between the homes. Farmers stepped into the fields carrying tools over their shoulders. Students gathered in small groups and walked toward the **Learning Hall**, their voices bright with conversation.

Near the center of town a baker opened the shutters of his small shop, allowing the warmth of the ovens to spill into the cool morning air. The scent of fresh grain bread drifted down the street as the first customers arrived.

It was the ordinary beginning of another day.

But not everyone in Valaryn had slept well the night before.

The Disturbance

Dr. **Arel Ziv** stood quietly beside the instrument table in his study.

The room was filled with pale morning light from a wide window overlooking the valley. Shelves lined the curved stone walls, holding rows of scientific texts, observation logs, and carefully organized journals.

The instruments on the central table still glowed faintly.

Ziv studied the display with thoughtful concentration.

Something unusual had occurred during the night.

A powerful disturbance had passed through the upper atmosphere—brief, intense, and highly localized.

He tapped the console again.

The sensors replayed the event in a thin glowing line across the display.

A sudden burst of energy.

A steep descent through the upper atmosphere.

Then silence.

Ziv leaned closer.

"Meteor?" he murmured to himself.

But the pattern did not behave like a natural impact. Meteors entered the atmosphere at predictable angles and scattered fragments as they burned.

This object had remained intact.

And it had changed course.

He adjusted the display again.

The trajectory formed a precise path across the sky.

Something had entered Cyrion's atmosphere at extraordinary speed.

And it had come down somewhere west of Valaryn.

Ziv frowned slightly.

That was not normal.

Lyara's Garden

Before leaving the house, Ziv stepped outside into the small garden behind the home.

Morning dew clung to the broad leaves of the **blueleaf plants**, each leaf catching the sunlight like polished glass. Tallroot vines climbed carefully along the stone wall where they had been trained over many seasons.

Ziv paused for a moment among the plants.

He did this every morning.

The garden had belonged to **Lyara**, his wife.

Though she had been gone for several years, the garden still carried her quiet presence. Ziv continued tending it carefully, planting new seeds each season and trimming the vines exactly the way she had once shown him.

He reached down and gently adjusted one of the climbing stems.

Lyara had always said the plants listened if you were patient enough to notice.

Ziv allowed himself a small smile.

"Still growing well," he said quietly.

The routine steadied his thoughts.

But today his attention drifted toward the horizon.

Somewhere beyond the distant ridges, the disturbance had occurred.

The sensors rarely made mistakes.

Something had fallen from the sky.

The Journey

Within the hour Ziv was traveling west across the valley in a small survey vehicle.

The vehicle moved smoothly over the uneven terrain, guided by magnetic tracks built into the stone pathways that connected Valaryn to the surrounding research stations.

The valley opened wide around him.

Fields stretched outward in gentle terraces where crops grew in long orderly rows. Beyond the cultivated land the terrain began to change. The green fields gave way to rugged stone and wind-carved formations rising from the earth like the ruins of ancient towers.

Beside him on the console, the atmospheric data continued to update.

The descent path remained clear.

Whatever had entered the atmosphere had come down hard.

Ziv felt his curiosity deepen.

Cyrion's skies were usually quiet.

Natural meteor impacts occurred from time to time, but the energy readings from the disturbance suggested something far more structured.

Something engineered.

The Valley Beyond

The path eventually left the cultivated lands of Valaryn and entered the open wilderness beyond the town.

Here the land felt older.

Stone formations rose higher, forming narrow passages where wind moved in low humming currents. Some pillars stretched hundreds of feet into the sky, their surfaces shaped by centuries of wind.

In the distance the tall columns of the **Talen Stone Forest** stood like silent giants.

Above them the twin moons of Cyrion faded slowly in the strengthening daylight.

A group of long-winged sky gliders passed overhead, riding the morning currents. Their shadows moved silently across the rocks below.

Ziv followed the sensor beacon deeper into the valley.

Then the signal spiked.

He slowed the vehicle.

The crash site was close.

The Wreckage

Ziv stepped out of the vehicle and walked forward cautiously.

At first he saw only broken stone and torn earth.

Then the metal appeared.

A massive structure lay half buried in the valley floor.

The surface of the object was scorched black from atmospheric entry. Large sections of its hull had split open during the impact, exposing twisted frameworks and shattered compartments inside.

Ziv stopped in silent amazement.

He had never seen a structure like this before.

The design was clearly artificial—sleek curves of metal formed from unfamiliar alloys that reflected the morning light with a dull silver sheen.

Not Cyrion technology.

This was technology from another world.

Not anything he recognized.

The crash had carved a long trench across the valley floor where the vessel had struck the ground and slid forward before finally coming to rest against a ridge of stone.

Smoke still drifted slowly from several openings in the wreckage.

Whatever had fallen from the sky had struck the valley with enormous force.

Inside the Ship

Ziv approached carefully and stepped through a jagged opening in the hull.

Inside, the air smelled of burned insulation and overheated circuitry.

Broken panels hung from the ceiling. Several compartments had collapsed inward during the crash, leaving piles of shattered equipment scattered across the floor.

Ziv moved slowly through the damaged compartments. Several passenger restraints had been torn loose during the impact. Others remained locked in place.

The silence inside the vessel told the story clearly enough.

The passengers had not survived the crash.

Ziv paused beside a control panel and activated the small transmitter in his survey vehicle.

"Valaryn Research Station," he said quietly. "This is Dr. Arel Ziv. I have located the source of the atmospheric disturbance. It is a spacecraft. Severe structural damage. Multiple fatalities."

He hesitated briefly before continuing.

"Recovery teams will be required."

The vessel was clearly some form of spacecraft.

He had studied theoretical designs of off-world vehicles during his research years, but this was the first time he had ever stood inside one.

Then he heard it.

A faint sound.

Small.

Almost too quiet to notice.

Ziv stopped and listened.

There it was again.

A soft cry.

The Discovery

He followed the sound deeper into the wreckage.

The corridor ended at a partially collapsed compartment where emergency lights still glowed faintly.

In the center of the room sat a small protective cradle.

Its emergency shielding had sealed automatically during the crash. Indicator lights still blinked steadily along its smooth surface.

Ziv approached slowly.

Inside the cradle, a tiny figure moved.

He knelt beside it.

The child looked up at him with wide, searching eyes.

For a moment neither of them moved.

Ziv studied the small face carefully.

This was not a Cyrion child.

The bone structure was different.

The skin lighter.

The proportions more delicate.

Ziv realized the truth almost immediately.

The structure he had found was not a meteor.

It was a ship.

And this child had been one of its passengers.

A Decision

Ziv gently opened the cradle's protective cover.

The child reached upward instinctively, gripping one of Ziv's fingers with surprising strength.

Ziv felt something shift quietly inside him.

He had come expecting to study an unusual atmospheric event.

Instead he had found a life.

A life that would not survive alone on Cyrion.

Ziv lifted the child carefully into his arms.

"You have traveled a very long way," he said softly.

The child blinked at him.

Ziv turned and looked out across the quiet valley.

The morning wind moved slowly across the tall grasses.

Somewhere far beyond the hills, the glowing plains of Cyrion waited for nightfall.

For a moment Ziv hesitated.

A child from another world would not easily survive on Cyrion. The gravity alone would challenge him.

But leaving the child here was not a choice.

Ziv looked down again at the small face in his arms.

"Well," he said quietly,

"It seems you are coming home with me."

Chapter 3 — Lyara's Garden

The road back to **Valaryn** wound gently through the valley.

Dr. Arel Ziv drove slowly, careful to avoid the deeper ruts in the stone path. The small survey vehicle moved quietly between tall grasses that bent and swayed in the morning wind.

The valley stretched wide around him.

Far to the east, the fields surrounding Valaryn lay in neat terraces of cultivated soil. Beyond them the rising stone formations cast long shadows across the land, their tall shapes glowing faintly in the growing light of Cyrion's sun.

In his arms, the child slept again.

Ziv had wrapped him carefully in the emergency blanket taken from the survival cradle. The reflective surface of the fabric had once been bright and clean, but now it was dulled by dust and ash from the wreckage.

Despite everything the child had endured, he seemed strangely peaceful.

Ziv glanced down at him from time to time as the vehicle moved across the valley floor.

Something about the child's proportions continued to draw Ziv's attention.

The infant's limbs were slimmer than those of a Cyrion newborn. The bone structure seemed lighter, almost delicate.

Ziv considered what that might mean.

If the ship truly came from another world, its passengers would have evolved under very different planetary conditions. Cyrion's gravity was far stronger than that of most habitable worlds studied in the astronomical records.

A child born elsewhere would grow differently here.

Ziv adjusted the blanket slightly around the sleeping infant.

"You may find this world a demanding teacher," he said quietly.

The small face remained calm.

No fear.

No distress.

Only sleep.

Ziv considered that quietly.

"You have chosen a difficult world," he murmured.

The child did not stir.

The vehicle continued forward along the winding stone road as the morning wind moved gently across the grasses of Cyrion.

Arrival in Valaryn

By the time Ziv reached the outskirts of Valaryn, the town had fully awakened.

People moved along the stone pathways between homes and gardens. Students crossed the central square on their way toward the **Learning Hall**, their voices bright with conversation.

Farmers were already tending the morning irrigation channels that carried water from the upper reservoirs down into the cultivated terraces.

The smell of warm grain bread drifted from a small bakery near the town square.

It was the ordinary rhythm of another day.

A few heads turned as Ziv's survey vehicle rolled slowly past.

The sight of their local scientist returning from an early field investigation was not unusual.

But the bundle he carried in his arms certainly was.

A pair of students slowed as they passed.

One of them whispered quietly.

"Is that a child?"

Ziv offered them a brief nod but did not stop.

Questions could wait.

He guided the vehicle down the final path that led to his home near the edge of town.

The small stone house sat slightly apart from the others, surrounded by low walls and shaded trees that Lyara had planted many years earlier.

A narrow path curved around the house and opened into a carefully tended garden behind the structure.

Ziv parked the vehicle and stepped out into the quiet morning air.

Then he carried the child toward the garden gate.

The Garden

The gate opened with a soft creak.

Inside, the air felt cooler.

Rows of **blueleaf plants** spread across the soil in wide clusters. Their broad leaves reflected soft shades of silver and blue in the sunlight. Tallroot vines climbed along the stone walls, their pale green tendrils curling patiently upward toward the warmth of the sun.

A narrow irrigation channel ran quietly through the center of the garden, feeding water to the roots of each plant.

The gentle sound of flowing water filled the quiet space.

Ziv paused for a moment.

He always did.

The garden had been Lyara's work.

Years earlier she had designed every section of it—each row arranged to catch the best sunlight, each plant chosen for its flavor or fragrance.

She had believed gardens should nourish both body and spirit.

After her death, Ziv had continued tending the garden carefully.

At first the work had been difficult. Every stone path, every vine, every small growing thing had carried the memory of her voice.

But over time the garden had become something else.

A quiet place of remembrance.

And peace.

Today, however, something about the garden felt different.

Ziv looked down at the child again.

Perhaps the house would not be quite so quiet anymore.

Inside the House

Ziv carried the child into the house and set him gently on a soft blanket placed across the central table.

The interior of the home was simple but warm.

Bookshelves lined one wall from floor to ceiling, filled with journals, research volumes, and carefully labeled field observations. Scientific instruments occupied a long workbench near the window.

A small dining table stood beside the kitchen alcove.

Sunlight filtered through the wide window that overlooked the garden, casting long bands of light across the wooden floor.

The child stirred.

His eyes opened slowly.

For a moment he seemed confused by the unfamiliar surroundings.

Then he looked directly at Ziv.

Ziv studied him thoughtfully.

"You appear to be remarkably resilient," he said quietly.

The child reached upward again, grasping Ziv's finger.

The grip was surprisingly strong.

Ziv raised one eyebrow slightly.

"Interesting."

Then he allowed himself a small smile.

The Name

Ziv activated a small handheld scanner and passed it gently over the child.

The device projected a faint display above its surface.

Several lines of unfamiliar symbols appeared.

Ziv adjusted the scanner's translation settings.

The system began converting the symbols slowly.

The device was reading the identification chip embedded in the survival cradle.

Ziv watched the translation carefully.

"William Arden."

He paused.

Then continued reading.

"William Arden… the second."

Ziv nodded thoughtfully.

"A long name for such a small traveler."

He looked down again at the child.

The baby blinked slowly, as though considering the situation.

"Perhaps we will begin with something simpler."

Ziv considered the name again.

"Bill," he said quietly.

The child made a small sound.

Ziv chose to interpret that as agreement.

"Yes," he said.

"Bill will do."

A New Routine

The morning passed quietly.

Ziv retrieved additional medical data from the survival cradle he had brought back from the wreckage. Using that information, he prepared a nutrient formula suitable for the child's biology.

Bill accepted the mixture eagerly.

Ziv took that as an encouraging sign.

Later, he carried the child outside again into the garden.

The sun had risen higher now, warming the stone walls and sending bright light across the valley beyond the house.

Bill watched the movement of the leaves overhead with quiet fascination.

The shifting patterns of sunlight seemed to capture his attention completely.

Ziv sat beside him on a low stone bench.

"You see," he said softly, gesturing toward the plants, "life here grows slowly."

The wind moved gently through the vines.

"Everything must learn to endure."

Bill stared upward at the shifting leaves, completely absorbed by the movement of light and shadow.

Ziv leaned back slightly and allowed himself a moment of quiet reflection.

Perhaps the child would learn.

The First Evening

As evening approached, the light across the valley began to soften.

The long shadows of the stone formations stretched slowly across the fields surrounding Valaryn.

Ziv carried Bill back outside one final time before nightfall.

The sky above Cyrion gradually darkened.

High overhead the first stars appeared.

Then the larger moon, **Selar**, rose slowly above the distant ridges.

Its pale light spread gently across the valley.

Bill looked upward with wide eyes.

Ziv followed his gaze.

"You will see many strange things here," he said quietly.

The child remained silent, watching the moon climb slowly into the sky.

Beyond the eastern hills, a faint glow began to spread along the horizon.

The **Lumar Plains** were beginning their nightly illumination.

Soft bands of pale light slowly brightened across the distant landscape.

Bill watched the glow with quiet wonder.

Ziv noticed the light and smiled slightly.

"It seems Cyrion wishes to welcome you properly."

He looked down again at the child.

For the first time since the crash, the scientist felt something he had not expected.

Hope.

Closing Image

Night settled gently over Valaryn.

In the quiet garden planted by Lyara, a small child slept peacefully beneath the twin moons of Cyrion.

The world that had taken so much from him had also given him something new.

A home.

And a man who would teach him how to live there.

Chapter 4 — A Difficult Choice

The first weeks passed quietly in Valaryn.

Bill adapted quickly to the rhythms of the small stone house. He slept often, ate eagerly, and watched everything around him with the silent curiosity common to young children.

Ziv soon noticed that the child preferred the garden.

Whenever the door opened, Bill's eyes followed the light spilling in from outside. The movement of leaves, the shifting shadows of the vines, and the gentle sound of flowing water from the irrigation channel seemed to fascinate him.

It was as if the child sensed that this small garden would become his first classroom on Cyrion.

Yet Dr. Arel Ziv noticed things others might have missed.

Subtle things.

Small signs that the child's body was struggling with the world around him.

The Weight of Cyrion

One morning Ziv placed Bill gently on a padded mat in the garden.

The air was cool and clear. The first light of Cyrion's sun filtered through the tallroot vines that climbed the garden wall.

Bill pushed himself upright using the low stone edge of a planting bed.

For a moment he balanced there, determined and proud.

Then his legs trembled.

The weight of Cyrion's gravity pressed down on him like an invisible hand.

Bill tried to take a step.

His foot lifted only slightly from the ground before dropping again.

He tried once more.

The result was the same.

The child's small arms strained as he tried to hold himself upright. His legs trembled with effort.

Ziv watched carefully.

The muscles were working exactly as they should.

But the force required to move them was simply too great.

Bill tried again.

His foot lifted a few centimeters.

Then he lost his balance and sat down heavily on the mat.

For a moment he looked startled.

Then frustrated.

Ziv knelt beside him.

"You are trying very hard," he said softly.

Bill looked up at him with confused determination.

Then he pushed himself upright again.

The effort lasted only a few seconds before exhaustion overtook him.

Ziv gently steadied the child and lowered him back onto the mat.

His expression remained calm.

But inside his mind, calculations had already begun.

The Scans

Later that afternoon Ziv returned to his laboratory.

The small room at the back of the house held several advanced medical instruments—tools he had used for years to study Cyrion biology.

Now they were focused on a different subject entirely.

A three-dimensional scan of Bill's brain floated above the diagnostic console.

Ziv studied it in silence.

The human brain was remarkable in many ways.

Flexible.

Creative.

Full of potential.

But on Cyrion it faced enormous challenges.

The planet's gravity demanded faster motor coordination. Its dense atmosphere required more efficient sensory processing. Its rugged terrain rewarded rapid pattern recognition and balance.

Bill's brain was healthy.

Exceptionally healthy.

But it was designed for a lighter world.

Ziv leaned back slowly in his chair.

Without intervention, Bill would always struggle.

Walking would be difficult.

Climbing almost impossible.

Even simple movement would require tremendous effort.

Perhaps the child would adapt partially.

But he would never move with the freedom of a Cyrion native.

Ziv folded his hands quietly.

And considered the future.

Lyara's Voice

He stepped outside again into the garden.

The afternoon light filtered through the leaves of the tallroot vines. The gentle wind carried the scent of growing plants across the small courtyard.

Bill slept peacefully on a blanket beneath the shade of the stone wall.

Ziv stood quietly for a long moment.

When Lyara had been alive, she often joined him in the garden during moments like this.

She had possessed a rare gift.

The ability to see problems clearly—and to remind him that knowledge was never separate from responsibility.

He rested his hand lightly on the stone wall she had built years earlier.

"Lyara," he said quietly, "what would you say now?"

The wind moved softly through the leaves.

There was no answer.

Yet somehow he felt he already knew it.

Lyara had always believed that knowledge carried an obligation.

If you had the ability to help someone survive…

You helped them.

The Possibility

Ziv returned to the laboratory and reopened the medical data.

There was one option.

A procedure developed decades earlier for Cyrion children suffering from severe neurological injury.

It was not designed to create superiority.

It did not add anything artificial to the brain.

Instead, it helped the brain organize itself more efficiently.

Neural signals traveled faster.

Sensory data processed more clearly.

Motor coordination improved.

The procedure simply allowed the brain to become the best version of itself.

For Cyrion children suffering from developmental damage, it had often meant the difference between life and death.

But it had never been attempted on a human.

Ziv stared at the display for a long time.

The risks were not insignificant.

Yet doing nothing carried its own consequences.

He closed his eyes briefly.

Then opened them again.

The decision had already formed.

The Decision

That evening he carried Bill into the laboratory.

The child was calm, watching the lights of the instruments with quiet fascination.

Ziv placed him gently into the stabilization cradle.

Soft restraints settled into place around the small body.

"You were not meant for this world," Ziv said quietly.

"But perhaps your mind can help you live here."

Bill reached toward him again.

His tiny fingers wrapped around Ziv's hand.

The same surprising strength.

Ziv felt the familiar tug in his chest.

Responsibility.

Compassion.

Hope.

He activated the medical system.

The room filled with the soft hum of delicate instruments.

The Enhancement

A network of microscopic bio-organic structures entered the child's neural system through a carefully controlled interface.

The process worked slowly and precisely.

Ziv monitored every signal.

Neural pathways strengthened.

Signal interference reduced.

Connections between sensory and motor centers refined.

The brain was not being replaced.

Only guided.

Encouraged to organize itself more effectively.

Minutes passed.

Then an hour.

The system continued its quiet work.

Finally a message appeared across the console.

Neural stabilization achieved.

Ziv exhaled slowly.

Afterward

He lifted the child gently from the cradle.

Bill blinked at him.

For a moment the child's eyes seemed unusually focused.

Alert.

Curious.

Almost as if he were studying the room with new clarity.

Ziv smiled faintly.

"Welcome to Cyrion," he said.

Closing Image

That night Ziv sat in the garden with the sleeping child beside him.

Above them the **Sky River** stretched across the stars like a pale band of light.

The twin moons of Cyrion rose slowly over the valley.

Ziv looked upward thoughtfully.

Perhaps the child would grow strong here.

Perhaps he would even thrive.

But strength alone would never be enough.

The world would test him in ways no child should face alone.

Ziv looked down at the sleeping boy.

"Strength grows slowly," he said quietly.

"And so does wisdom."

The wind moved gently through Lyara's garden.

And somewhere in the quiet valley of Valaryn, the first chapter of a very unusual life had begun.

Chapter 5 — The First Steps

Spring came slowly to the valley of **Valaryn**.

The mornings were cool and bright, and a gentle wind moved through the stone ridges surrounding the town. Thin clouds drifted across the wide blue sky while sunlight spread gradually across the fields below.

In **Lyara's garden**, new growth pushed upward through the dark soil.

Blueleaf plants spread wide along the irrigation channel, their broad leaves catching the light like polished glass. Tallroot vines climbed steadily along the stone wall, their tendrils reaching patiently toward the warmth of the sun.

The quiet sound of water flowing through the narrow irrigation channel filled the garden.

Dr. **Arel Ziv** knelt beside one of the planting beds, loosening the soil around a cluster of young stems.

Behind him a small figure watched with careful attention.

Bill sat on the low stone path, studying every movement Ziv made.

His eyes followed the slow rhythm of the work.

The way Ziv lifted the soil.

The way he brushed dirt away from the base of the plant.

The way he gently straightened the small stems so they would grow upright.

Bill watched everything.

Watching and Learning

The child had grown stronger in the months since Ziv had brought him home.

He could crawl now—slowly but with determination—and he spent much of his time exploring the small house and the garden outside.

Cyrion's gravity still pressed heavily on his body.

Every movement required effort.

When he crawled across the stone floor of the house, his arms trembled slightly under the constant pull of the planet.

Yet Bill never seemed discouraged by the difficulty.

Instead, he watched.

Carefully.

Patiently.

Just as Ziv had begun teaching him.

When Ziv worked in the garden, Bill watched.

When Ziv studied his instruments in the laboratory, Bill watched.

When Ziv sat quietly in the evening and looked toward the stars, Bill watched that too.

The child seemed determined to understand the world around him.

The Attempt

That morning something new caught Ziv's attention.

Bill had pulled himself upright using the edge of the stone wall.

The effort had taken several tries, but now he stood there, gripping the rough stone with both hands.

His small arms trembled.

Ziv remained where he was.

He did not move closer.

Some lessons had to unfold naturally.

Bill shifted his weight slightly.

His legs trembled beneath him.

For a moment he looked uncertain.

Then he lifted one foot.

The Weight of the World

The step should have been simple.

On Earth it would have been effortless.

But on Cyrion the planet itself seemed to resist him.

Gravity pressed downward like an invisible hand.

Bill's foot barely cleared the ground.

He placed it forward carefully.

One step.

Ziv watched quietly.

Bill tried another.

This time his legs shook more violently.

The effort was enormous for such a small body.

The muscles in his legs strained as though he were carrying a heavy load.

Ziv felt a quiet sense of admiration.

The child had not yet learned the word **impossible**.

The Fall

Bill attempted a third step.

His balance shifted.

The weight of Cyrion pulled him sideways.

He fell heavily onto the soft soil of the garden bed.

For a moment he lay still.

Then he looked up at Ziv.

His expression showed confusion more than pain.

The child had expected the world to cooperate.

Instead, it had knocked him down.

Encouragement

Ziv stood and walked over to him.

He knelt beside the small figure and brushed the loose soil from Bill's sleeve.

"You did well," he said calmly.

Bill stared at him for a moment.

Then he turned back toward the stone wall.

Slowly he pushed himself upright again.

Ziv watched quietly.

"Very well," he murmured.

Again and Again

The process repeated itself throughout the morning.

Bill stood.

Took a step.

Then fell.

Each attempt lasted only seconds before the weight of the planet forced him back to the ground.

But the child never stopped trying.

Several times he paused to rest, breathing heavily from the effort.

Then he crawled back to the stone wall and tried again.

Ziv sat nearby on a low stone bench, quietly observing.

Occasionally he offered a steady hand when Bill stood.

But he never carried him away from the effort.

Learning to live on Cyrion would require patience.

And courage.

Both would grow stronger only through practice.

The Lesson

By midday the child was exhausted.

Bill sat beside the irrigation channel, staring at the flowing water.

The small stream moved slowly along the carved stone path, reflecting the bright light of the sun.

His breathing came in small tired bursts.

Ziv sat beside him.

For a moment neither of them spoke.

The garden was quiet except for the wind moving softly through the leaves.

Ziv pointed gently toward the tallroot vines climbing the garden wall.

"Those plants began smaller than you," he said.

Bill followed his gaze.

"They grow slowly."

The wind rustled through the leaves above them.

Ziv rested a hand lightly on the child's shoulder.

"Strength grows slowly."

Bill did not fully understand the words yet.

But he listened.

And the calm certainty in Ziv's voice seemed to settle something inside him.

A Small Victory

Late that afternoon Bill stood again.

The shadows of the garden wall stretched longer across the soil.

The air had grown cooler.

This time he took one step.

Then another.

Three steps in a row before the familiar pull of gravity sent him tumbling forward.

He landed in the soil beside the blueleaf plants.

Ziv laughed softly.

Bill looked up at him in surprise.

Then he laughed too.

The sound echoed gently across the garden.

Closing Image

As evening settled over Valaryn, the two of them remained in the garden.

The sky darkened slowly.

Above the valley the first stars appeared.

Bill leaned against Ziv's knee, watching the lights in the sky.

He was too tired to try walking again that day.

But tomorrow he would.

And the day after that.

And the day after that.

Years later, when the people of Valaryn watched the young man climb the towering pillars of the **Stone Forest**, they would see strength and balance in every movement.

Only Dr. Arel Ziv would remember the small boy who once struggled to take three steps in a garden.

And refused to give up.

Chapter 6 — The Light Beyond the Valley

The seasons on **Cyrion** changed more slowly than on many human worlds.

Spring lingered in the valley of **Valaryn**, bringing longer days and gentle winds that moved across the hills like quiet waves. The gardens surrounding the town were full now, with vines climbing the stone walls and wide leaves spreading across the fertile soil.

Fields beyond the town had begun their slow seasonal growth. Farmers worked the terraces early each morning, guiding water along the irrigation channels that fed the valley's crops.

Life in Valaryn followed the same steady rhythm it had known for generations.

But in **Lyara's garden**, something new had begun to grow.

Bill had grown stronger.

He could walk now—carefully and with effort—but the heavy gravity of Cyrion no longer forced him to the ground every few steps. His movements were still slower than those of Cyrion children, but they were steady.

Each step was deliberate.

Balanced.

Determined.

Dr. **Arel Ziv** often watched him cross the garden path with quiet satisfaction.

Strength, after all, grew slowly.

And Bill seemed willing to give the process all the time it required.

An Evening Question

One evening Bill sat beside Ziv on the low stone bench near the edge of the garden.

The air had cooled after the long afternoon, and the first hints of evening were beginning to settle across the valley.

The sun had just slipped behind the western ridges, leaving long shadows stretching across the fields.

Bill looked toward the eastern horizon.

Something there caught his attention.

A faint glow.

At first he thought it might be the last reflection of sunset, but the light was different.

It shimmered softly.

And it was spreading.

Slowly the distant plains began to brighten.

Bill leaned forward.

"What is that?"

Ziv followed his gaze.

He smiled.

"The **Lumar Plains**," he said.

Bill continued watching.

"They're shining."

"Yes," Ziv replied.

"They always do after sunset."

Bill tilted his head slightly, studying the distant glow as if trying to understand how land itself could produce light.

The Walk

Ziv stood and gestured toward the narrow path that climbed the ridge behind the garden.

"Come," he said.

Bill followed him slowly up the slope.

The path curved upward between clusters of tall grasses and smooth stone outcrops. It was not steep, but under Cyrion's gravity the climb still required effort.

Bill paused once or twice along the way.

Each time he placed his hands on his knees and took several deep breaths.

Ziv waited patiently.

He never hurried him.

Eventually they reached the top of the ridge.

And the view opened wide before them.

The Valley of Valaryn

From the ridge the entire valley could be seen.

The town of Valaryn rested quietly among its gardens and orchards, its stone houses catching the last faint light of evening.

Thin trails of smoke rose from a few chimneys as families prepared their evening meals.

Beyond the cultivated land the valley widened into open plains.

And across those plains the strange glow had grown brighter.

Bill stepped forward.

The Lumar Plains

He stopped walking.

The sight before him held his attention completely.

The plains were covered with millions of small moss-like plants that gathered energy during the day. As darkness fell, the plants released that energy slowly, producing a soft blue-green light.

From the ridge the effect was breathtaking.

The land looked like a silent ocean of light.

Waves of illumination moved gently across the plains as the evening wind brushed the surface of the glowing moss.

Bill stared in wonder.

"It looks alive," he whispered.

Ziv nodded.

"In a way, it is."

Bill watched the slow movement of the glowing waves.

"How far does it go?"

"Farther than you can see," Ziv said.

Bill tried to imagine that.

The Sky Above

As the last light of day faded, the sky above them deepened into a rich blue.

Then the first stars appeared.

One.

Then another.

Soon the bright band of the Sky River stretched across the heavens like a glowing path among the stars.

Bill looked up at it.

"So many," he said quietly.

Ziv sat beside him on the ridge.

"Yes.

The universe is very large."

Bill lay back on the cool grass and stared upward.

He had seen the stars before from the garden.

But from the ridge the sky seemed larger.

Deeper.

Almost endless.

"Are there other worlds?" Bill asked.

Ziv looked up at the stars for a long moment.

"Yes," he said.

"There are many."

Bill was quiet for a while.

Then he asked a second question.

"Did people come from there?"

Ziv turned his head slightly and looked at the child beside him.

"Yes."

Earlier that evening, Ziv had carefully explained to Bill how the damaged vessel had fallen from the sky and how the small survivor inside it had come to live in his home.

Bill had listened quietly.

Now he nodded slowly.

That answer seemed to settle something inside him.

A Lesson

Bill eventually looked back toward the glowing plains.

"Did the plains always shine like that?" he asked.

"Yes," Ziv replied.

"They have done so for thousands of years."

Bill thought about that.

"So they will shine tomorrow too?"

Ziv smiled.

"Yes."

Bill seemed satisfied with that answer.

The glowing plains continued their slow shimmering movement far below the ridge.

Ziv rested his hands on the ground beside him.

"Some things," he said quietly, "remain steady for a very long time."

Bill watched the glowing landscape again.

He did not fully understand the meaning of the words yet.

But he listened.

Closing Image

Later, as they walked back down toward the garden, Bill looked over his shoulder one more time.

The glowing plains stretched across the dark landscape beneath the rising moon.

The quiet waves of light moved gently across the land.

For the first time since arriving on Cyrion, the strange planet no longer felt entirely unfamiliar.

It felt…

Beautiful.

And though he did not yet have the words to express it, something quiet had begun to grow inside him.

A sense that this world might one day feel like home.

Chapter 7 — The Young Varik

The hills beyond **Valaryn** were quiet in the early morning.

Mist drifted slowly between the tall stone pillars that marked the beginning of the **Talen Stone Forest**, and the first light of Cyrion's sun touched the upper edges of the rocks like a pale crown of gold.

The air carried the cool scent of stone and grass.

Bill walked carefully along the narrow trail that led away from the town.

He was older now.

Stronger too.

His legs had grown steady under the heavy gravity of Cyrion, and though he still moved more slowly than the native people of the planet, he no longer stumbled with every step.

His stride had become deliberate.

Balanced.

Confident.

Behind him the valley of Valaryn lay quiet beneath the morning sun. Thin threads of smoke rose from the chimneys of the town as families began their daily routines.

Ahead of him stretched the hills and the tall stone formations of the wilderness.

Each day Bill explored a little farther.

Each day the world grew larger.

A Strange Sound

Bill stopped suddenly.

Something had moved among the tall grasses beside the path.

He listened carefully.

The wind shifted through the stems with a soft whisper.

Then he heard it again.

A low sound.

Soft.

Uneven.

Not the quick rustling of a small grazing animal.

And not the high call of the valley birds.

This sound carried something else.

Pain.

Bill stepped slowly toward the grass.

The Discovery

At first he saw only movement.

Then the creature lifted its head.

Bill froze.

The animal was larger than any creature he had seen so close before—about the size of the small riding animals used by farmers in the valley.

Its body was covered in thick gray-blue fur that shifted in the morning light. A ridge of darker hair ran along its spine, giving the creature a slightly wild appearance.

Two bright amber eyes watched him carefully.

The creature attempted to stand.

Its front legs pushed against the ground.

Its body rose halfway.

Then it collapsed again.

Bill immediately noticed the problem.

One of the animal's hind legs was twisted awkwardly beneath it.

The creature gave a low, frustrated sound.

It was injured.

Fear and Trust

For a moment neither of them moved.

The creature watched Bill with wary caution.

Its breathing was quick.

Bill remembered Ziv's words.

Observe first.

Act second.

He crouched slowly, lowering himself toward the ground so he would appear less threatening.

The animal's ears twitched.

Its muscles tightened slightly as if preparing to flee.

But it could not run.

Bill extended his hand slowly.

"I won't hurt you," he said softly.

The creature made a low rumbling sound deep in its chest.

Bill remained completely still.

The wind moved through the grass around them.

After several moments the animal's breathing slowed.

A Careful Approach

Bill moved closer.

The creature watched him carefully but did not retreat.

He examined the injured leg.

The wound was not a break.

But a sharp stone had cut the muscle near the joint, leaving the animal unable to support its weight.

Bill glanced around.

A small stream ran nearby between the rocks.

He moved toward it slowly and filled a large folded leaf with water.

When he returned, the creature watched him with quiet attention.

Bill gently cleaned the wound.

The animal flinched slightly but did not pull away.

"Easy," Bill murmured.

The water washed away the dried blood and dust.

After cleaning the wound, Bill tore a strip from the cloth he carried over his shoulder and wrapped the injured leg as best he could.

The creature watched every movement.

Its amber eyes never left his face.

The First Bond

When Bill finished, he sat back on the grass.

"You'll need to rest," he said quietly.

The creature lowered its head.

Its breathing had become slower now.

Calmer.

For several minutes they remained there together in silence.

The wind moved through the grass.

A distant bird called somewhere high among the stone pillars.

Then the animal slowly crawled closer.

It sniffed Bill's hand.

Bill did not move.

After a moment the creature rested its head gently against his knee.

Bill smiled.

The Journey Home

The sun had climbed higher by the time Bill finally stood.

He began the slow walk back toward Valaryn.

The Varik followed behind him.

At first it moved cautiously, placing little weight on the injured leg.

But the bandage held, and with each careful step the animal seemed more confident.

From time to time Bill looked back to make sure the creature was still following.

It always was.

Ziv's Explanation

Later that afternoon Bill reached the garden gate with his unusual companion walking slowly behind him.

Dr. **Arel Ziv** looked up from the garden path as they approached.

His eyebrows lifted slightly.

"Well," he said calmly,

"that is not something we see every day."

Bill pointed toward the bandaged leg.

"It was hurt."

Ziv walked slowly around the animal, studying it with professional curiosity.

The Varik watched him with alert caution but did not move away.

"A **Varik**," Ziv said at last.

The creature lifted its head slightly, as though acknowledging the name.

Ziv nodded.

"An intelligent species," he continued.

"Strong, patient, and loyal once trust is given."

He glanced toward Bill.

"It seems you have already earned that trust."

A Name

That evening the Varik rested beside the garden wall while Bill sat nearby.

The creature watched him closely.

Its amber eyes reflected the fading light of sunset.

"What should I call you?" Bill wondered aloud.

The animal tilted its head slightly.

Bill thought for a moment.

Then he smiled.

"**Ruun**," he said.

The Varik's ears twitched gently.

The name seemed to please it.

Closing Image

Night fell gently across the valley.

The two moons of Cyrion rose slowly above the distant hills.

In **Lyara's garden**, beneath the quiet glow of the stars, a boy sat beside the first creature who had chosen him as a friend.

The bond between them had begun quietly.

But in the years ahead, the people of Valaryn would often see the two of them together.

The human boy who struggled to keep pace with their world.

And the loyal Varik who never left his side.

Chapter 8 — The Children of Valaryn

Morning sunlight filled the central square of **Valaryn**.

The stone courtyard stretched wide between the buildings of the town's learning district. Tall pillars surrounded the open space, their pale surfaces reflecting the bright light of Cyrion's rising sun.

Students gathered outside the **Learning Hall**, their voices rising and falling in the easy rhythm of conversation.

The hall itself stood at the far side of the square, its wide entrance framed by carved stone arches. Inside, teachers prepared the day's lessons while the children lingered outside, enjoying the cool air of the morning.

Bill stood near the edge of the square.

Beside him sat **Ruun**, the young Varik, watching the activity with quiet interest.

The creature's amber eyes followed the movement of the children as they crossed the courtyard.

Bill had been visiting the Learning Hall for several weeks now.

Dr. **Arel Ziv** believed it was important for him to hear the language of Cyrion spoken regularly.

"Understanding comes from listening," Ziv had said.

Bill had taken the advice seriously.

Whenever he visited the square, he listened carefully.

Every word.

Every tone.

Every pattern in the way people spoke to one another.

Language, he had discovered, was not only about words.

It was about people.

Different

The children of Valaryn were taller than Bill.

Even those close to his age seemed stronger, their movements quick and effortless under Cyrion's gravity.

They ran across the courtyard with easy balance while Bill walked more carefully, measuring each step.

A few children noticed him standing near the pillars.

Some whispered quietly.

Others simply stared with open curiosity.

A boy about Bill's age stepped forward.

His name was **Soren**.

"You are the human," he said.

Bill nodded.

"Yes."

Soren studied him without hesitation.

"You move slowly."

Bill considered the observation carefully.

"Yes," he replied again.

Soren shrugged.

"That is because this world is heavy."

Bill could not argue with that.

Watching the Game

The children soon returned to their game in the center of the courtyard.

They were throwing a small stone disk between the pillars, running quickly to catch it before it struck the ground.

The rules seemed simple.

But the speed of the game was remarkable.

Players moved swiftly across the stone floor, predicting where the disk would fall before it reached the ground.

Bill watched them carefully.

Every movement fascinated him.

Each throw followed a pattern.

Each player adjusted their position before the disk even reached its highest point.

They were not simply reacting.

They were predicting.

Ruun sat beside him, quietly observing as well.

The Varik's ears twitched with interest each time the disk struck the stone.

An Invitation

Finally one of the children called out.

"Do you want to try?"

Several heads turned toward Bill.

He hesitated.

The game moved quickly.

Too quickly.

But the invitation had been offered.

Bill nodded.

The Attempt

Soren tossed the disk gently toward him.

Bill reached for it.

But the weight of Cyrion slowed his movement.

The disk struck the ground before he could catch it.

A few children laughed—not cruelly, but with the easy amusement of those who had never struggled with such simple things.

Bill picked up the disk and handed it back.

"Try again," Soren said.

Bill studied the disk carefully.

Then he nodded.

Learning

This time Bill did something different.

Instead of focusing on the disk alone, he watched the players.

Their feet.

Their shoulders.

The direction of their movement.

When the next throw came, Bill moved earlier.

His hand closed around the disk just before it reached the ground.

The children stopped.

"That was better," Soren admitted.

Bill allowed himself a small smile.

Observation

The game continued.

Bill missed many throws.

Sometimes the disk struck the ground before he even began to move.

But he caught a few as well.

Each success came because he watched closely and adjusted his timing.

He began predicting the throws just as the others did.

By the end of the game the children had stopped laughing.

They had begun to notice something.

The human boy might move slowly.

But he learned quickly.

Ruun's Moment

At one point the disk rolled toward the edge of the courtyard.

Before anyone could reach it, **Ruun** bounded forward.

The Varik moved with sudden speed, scooping the disk up in his mouth.

He trotted proudly back to Bill and dropped the disk at his feet.

The children stared.

Then several of them laughed.

Soren shook his head.

"Well," he said, "your friend is faster than you."

Bill scratched Ruun behind the ear.

"That is true."

Ruun wagged his thick tail in quiet satisfaction.

A Quiet Respect

The game eventually ended.

The children gathered their things and began returning to the Learning Hall.

Soren paused beside Bill.

"You will improve," he said.

Bill looked at him.

"How do you know?"

Soren gestured toward the garden path that led out of the town.

"I have seen you walking there every morning."

Bill nodded slowly.

"Yes."

"You fall," Soren continued.

Bill did not deny it.

"But you always stand up again."

Soren shrugged.

"That is how strength grows."

Bill considered those words carefully.

They sounded strangely familiar.

Closing Image

Later that day Bill walked home beside Dr. Ziv.

Ruun trotted ahead of them along the path, occasionally stopping to investigate something interesting among the grasses.

"How did the lessons go?" Ziv asked.

Bill thought for a moment.

"I am still slower than they are."

Ziv nodded.

"That may always be true."

Bill watched the children playing in the distance as they passed the Learning Hall.

"But they did not laugh at the end."

Ziv smiled gently.

"That is often the beginning of respect."

They continued walking through the quiet streets of Valaryn as the afternoon sun drifted slowly toward the western ridges.

Bill felt tired.

But he also felt something new.

The quiet sense that perhaps—

slowly—

he was beginning to belong.

Chapter 9 — The Day of the Trial

The morning of the **First Trial** arrived with clear skies over Valaryn.

The valley was unusually busy.

People moved along the stone paths toward the open training grounds on the northern edge of town. Families walked together beneath the tall pillars that marked the older part of the settlement, their voices filling the air with anticipation.

The **Trials of Youth** were not held every year.

But when they were, the entire community gathered to watch.

For the children of Cyrion, the Trials marked an important step toward adulthood.

Strength.

Balance.

Endurance.

The three qualities every citizen of Cyrion was expected to develop.

Bill walked slowly beside **Dr. Arel Ziv** along the path leading toward the gathering field.

Beside them trotted **Ruun**, the young Varik, his ears alert to every sound.

"You do not have to participate," Ziv said quietly.

Bill kept walking.

"I know."

The Trial Grounds

The training grounds lay just beyond the northern edge of the town.

Tall stone pillars surrounded the open field, forming a natural arena that had been used for generations. The pillars were older than Valaryn itself, carved long ago by the first settlers who had chosen this valley as their home.

Between the pillars stood wooden platforms, climbing frames, and balance structures built among the stone.

These were the obstacles used in the Trials.

Children from the **Learning Hall** gathered near the starting line.

Some stretched their arms and legs.

Others laughed nervously as they waited.

Parents and elders stood along the edges of the field, watching quietly.

Bill stood slightly apart from the other participants.

Everyone present understood the difficulty he faced.

Cyrion's gravity alone made the challenge enormous.

Several adults glanced toward him with quiet curiosity.

The human child had chosen to stand among the participants.

Few expected him to succeed.

The First Test

The instructor stepped forward.

He was a tall man with gray hair and the calm posture of someone who had led many Trials before.

"The First Trial," he announced, "is the climb."

He gestured toward the stone wall rising at the far edge of the field.

The climb consisted of a series of natural stone ledges carved into the face of one of the larger pillars.

Twenty feet above the ground, the final platform waited.

For Cyrion children the climb required strength and coordination.

For Bill, it required nearly everything he had.

The instructor raised his hand.

"Begin."

The Climb Begins

The children rushed forward.

They climbed quickly, pulling themselves upward along the carved handholds in the stone.

Some moved with practiced ease, their bodies already adapted to the heavy gravity of their world.

Bill followed.

Slowly.

Each movement demanded careful effort.

He placed his hands deliberately on the first stone ledge.

Then he pulled.

The weight of Cyrion pressed against his arms like an invisible force.

Below him Ruun paced nervously near the edge of the field.

Several children reached the second ledge before Bill had fully pulled himself onto the first.

But he did not stop.

He continued climbing.

The Weight of the World

The second ledge required even greater effort.

Bill tightened his grip and lifted himself upward.

His arms trembled.

The muscles in his shoulders strained beneath the weight of his own body.

He paused briefly on the narrow ledge.

Below him the watching crowd had grown silent.

No one laughed.

No one spoke.

They simply watched.

Bill reached for the next handhold.

The Slip

Halfway up the wall Bill's hand lost its grip.

His foot slipped against the rough stone.

For a moment he dangled from one arm.

The weight of the planet dragged heavily at his body.

Gasps rose from the watching crowd.

Ruun barked sharply from the ground below.

Bill's arm trembled.

But he did not let go.

With a deep breath he swung his other arm upward.

His fingers found the next handhold.

Slowly—inch by inch—he pulled himself onto the ledge.

The climb continued.

The Final Platform

By the time Bill reached the final platform, the other children had already finished the climb.

Some stood waiting at the top.

Others had already descended to the ground.

Bill stood there breathing heavily.

His arms trembled with exhaustion.

Sweat ran down his face.

But he had reached the top.

The instructor looked up at him and nodded respectfully.

"You finished," he said.

Bill climbed down carefully.

Each step downward felt heavier than the last.

But when his feet finally touched the ground, Ruun bounded forward happily.

The Lesson

As the Trials continued with other challenges, Bill sat beside Ziv near the edge of the field.

His arms still trembled slightly from the effort.

"You climbed farther than most expected," Ziv said.

Bill watched the other children completing their runs and jumps.

"They were faster."

"Yes."

Bill considered that.

"But I finished."

Ziv smiled.

"That is often more important."

The Elder's Observation

Later that afternoon, as the crowd slowly dispersed, one of the elders approached them.

The man was tall and carried the quiet authority of someone who had lived many years in the valley.

He studied Bill thoughtfully.

"You are not built like our children," he said.

Bill nodded.

"That is true."

"But you climb anyway."

Bill glanced back toward the stone wall.

"Yes."

The elder considered this for a moment.

Then he nodded once and turned away.

He did not say anything more.

But several others had watched the moment carefully.

The human boy had attempted a trial that even some Cyrion children avoided.

And he had finished.

Closing Image

That evening Bill and Ruun sat beside the garden wall while the last light faded from the valley.

His arms still ached from the climb.

But his mind replayed the moment again and again.

The ledge.

The slip.

The pull upward.

Above them the stars began to appear.

Bill looked toward the distant hills beyond Valaryn.

Someday he would climb higher than that wall.

Someday he would move across Cyrion as confidently as the people who had been born there.

For now, it was enough to know one thing.

He had begun.

Chapter 10 — The Night of the Storm

The air felt different that afternoon.

Even before the clouds appeared, the people of **Valaryn** sensed the change.

The wind carried a faint metallic scent across the valley. It moved through the grasses in slow restless waves, bending the tall stems in uneven patterns.

High above the stone ridges the birds that usually circled the valley had vanished into the shelter of the cliffs.

The sky remained clear.

But the stillness beneath it felt uneasy.

Dr. **Arel Ziv** noticed the change while working in **Lyara's garden**.

He had been tending the irrigation channel when the wind shifted.

He stood slowly and looked toward the western horizon.

Beyond the distant ridges, the sky had begun to darken.

Bill followed his gaze.

"Is it going to rain?" he asked.

Ziv studied the horizon a moment longer.

Then he shook his head.

"Something stronger."

The Warning

By early evening the entire valley had grown unusually quiet.

Farmers working the outer terraces packed their tools and secured the irrigation gates that carried water into the fields.

Market stalls folded their coverings.

Merchants carried their goods inside the stone buildings that lined the central square.

Children were called home.

Across the valley doors closed and shutters were fastened.

Bill helped Ziv secure the wooden panels along the garden wall.

The air had grown heavy and still.

"What kind of storm is it?" Bill asked.

Ziv glanced once more toward the darkening sky.

"A **Storm Wall**."

Bill had heard the words before.

The elders sometimes spoke of them when discussing the seasons.

But he had never seen one.

Gathering Clouds

As the sun sank toward the western ridges, the sky began to change.

What had first appeared to be distant clouds now formed a thick dark line across the horizon.

The line slowly widened.

Above it lightning flickered silently.

Bill stood beside the garden gate, watching.

The line continued to grow taller.

And darker.

"What is it doing?" he asked quietly.

"It is building strength," Ziv said.

Storm Walls did not arrive suddenly.

They gathered.

Slowly.

Patiently.

Like a tide rising across the sky.

The Arrival

Night had just begun to fall when the storm finally revealed its full shape.

The distant dark line began to move.

At first the movement was subtle.

Then it became unmistakable.

A towering wall of wind and lightning swept across the plains like a moving mountain.

From Valaryn it looked enormous.

The storm stretched from one end of the valley to the other.

Lightning flashed through its dark center, illuminating vast rolling clouds of dust and rain.

Bill stared in awe.

"It's huge," he whispered.

Ziv nodded.

"Yes."

Storm Walls were among the most powerful natural forces on Cyrion.

Even the oldest settlements respected them.

The Sound

For several moments the storm advanced in silence.

Then the sound arrived.

A deep rolling roar spread across the valley.

The wind struck the outer stone ridges first.

The impact echoed between the cliffs like distant thunder.

The town's protective wind barriers began to hum under the pressure.

Bill felt the vibration through the ground beneath his feet.

The stone beneath the garden wall trembled faintly.

Beside him **Ruun** pressed close, ears flattened against his head.

The Varik's instincts recognized danger.

Inside the House

Ziv placed a steady hand on Bill's shoulder.

"Come inside."

They stepped into the house as the first heavy gusts of wind swept through the valley.

Ziv secured the final window shutters and dimmed the interior lights.

Outside the wind began to rise.

Dust swept across the valley floor in swirling clouds.

Lightning illuminated the sky again and again.

The flashes lit the stone walls of the house in sharp white bursts.

"Storm Walls are powerful," Ziv explained calmly.

"But Valaryn has faced many of them."

The stone houses had been built with thick walls and narrow windows.

The town itself had been positioned carefully between protective ridges.

Bill listened to the storm growing stronger outside.

The Heart of the Storm

Nearly an hour later the Storm Wall reached the valley.

The wind struck the outer ridges with tremendous force.

Trees bent low against the pressure.

Rain hammered against the stone walls of the house like thousands of thrown pebbles.

The roar of the wind filled the valley.

Bill sat beside the window, listening.

The power of the storm fascinated him.

The wind howled like a living creature moving across the land.

Lightning split the sky above the valley again and again.

For a moment the entire world seemed made of light and thunder.

Ruun paced nervously across the floor.

The Lesson

Ziv sat beside Bill.

"Cyrion is a strong world," he said quietly.

Bill nodded.

"Yes."

"But strength is not something we conquer."

Bill turned toward him.

Ziv gestured toward the storm raging outside.

"We respect it."

Bill watched another flash of lightning spread across the sky.

He understood.

The Passing

Gradually the wind began to weaken.

The roar softened to a distant rumble as the Storm Wall moved east across the **Lumar Plains**.

Rain continued to fall for a while longer.

Then even that softened.

The valley slowly grew quiet again.

Ziv opened the door and stepped outside.

Bill followed.

After the Storm

The air smelled fresh and clean.

Water ran through the irrigation channels, filling the garden beds with new moisture.

Drops of rain clung to the leaves of the blueleaf plants.

Above them the clouds slowly parted.

Stars appeared once more in the dark sky.

Far in the distance the Storm Wall continued its journey across the plains.

Its lightning flickered faintly along the horizon.

Closing Image

Ruun bounded happily through the wet grass, shaking rain from his thick fur.

Bill stood beside Ziv near the garden wall.

"That storm was stronger than anything I've ever seen," Bill said.

Ziv smiled gently.

"You have lived here only a short time."

Bill looked toward the distant horizon where the last flashes of lightning faded.

"Will they always be that powerful?"

Ziv nodded.

"Yes."

Bill thought about that for a moment.

Then he said quietly,

"Someday I want to understand them."

Ziv looked down at the boy with quiet interest.

"Perhaps," he said,

"you will."

Above them the stars of the **Sky River** stretched across the heavens once more.

And somewhere far beyond the valley, the Storm Wall continued its long journey across the glowing plains of Cyrion.

Chapter 11 — The Library of Valaryn

The **Library of Valaryn** stood near the center of town, not far from the Learning Hall.

It was one of the oldest buildings in the valley.

Unlike many of the newer stone homes that had been built with smooth walls and modern materials, the library had been carved directly into the side of a low ridge centuries earlier. Tall pillars framed its entrance, and wide steps led upward to a set of heavy doors made from polished **stonewood**.

The doors alone had stood for generations.

Many of the elders of Valaryn remembered walking through them as children.

To the people of the valley, the library was more than a place for books.

It was a place for memory.

For generations the knowledge of Cyrion had been gathered there—scientific records, agricultural studies, star charts, histories of the valley, and the preserved writings of scholars who had lived long before the current town existed.

Some of the oldest texts dated back to the earliest settlers who had first arrived on Cyrion.

Dr. **Arel Ziv** had visited the library for most of his life.

But the person who now visited most often was **Bill**.

A Place of Quiet

Bill pushed open the heavy door and stepped inside.

The familiar scent of aged paper and polished wood filled the air.

The chamber was enormous.

Rows of shelves stretched across the wide hall, their surfaces lined with books, data tablets, and storage crystals containing centuries of recorded knowledge.

Tall windows near the ceiling allowed thin beams of sunlight to fall across the reading tables below.

Dust drifted slowly through the light like tiny floating stars.

The room was quiet.

Bill liked that.

In the quiet, his thoughts felt clearer.

And there were always new things to learn.

A New Kind of Work

Several months earlier, the librarian had offered him a small job.

The position was simple.

Organizing returned books.

Cleaning the reading tables.

Carrying stacks of records between the archive rooms and the main hall.

For most of the children of Valaryn, such work would have seemed dull.

But for Bill it opened an entirely new world.

Every shelf contained stories.

Every record contained ideas.

Books were windows into places he had never seen.

And there were many places he had never seen.

Learning to Learn

At first Bill struggled with the written language.

Though he had grown fluent in spoken Cyrion speech, the written form contained complex structures and layered meanings that required patience to understand.

But patience had become one of Bill's greatest strengths.

Each day he studied new words.

Each day the symbols on the page became clearer.

The neural enhancements Ziv had given him allowed his mind to recognize patterns quickly, but the deeper understanding still required time.

Soon he was reading not only the children's learning texts but also historical records and scientific studies.

The librarians noticed.

Few students his age showed such focus.

Fewer still asked such thoughtful questions.

Tarin Sol

The head librarian, **Tarin Sol**, had watched his progress carefully.

She was a quiet woman with silver hair and thoughtful eyes that seemed to notice everything in the room at once.

One afternoon she approached Bill while he was shelving a stack of returned volumes.

"You read more than most of the students who come here," she observed.

Bill placed another book on the shelf.

"I like learning."

Tarin smiled slightly.

"That is fortunate."

She studied him for a moment.

"There is another room you may find interesting."

Bill looked up.

"What kind of room?"

"The **Archive Hall**."

She gestured toward a narrow corridor behind the main chamber.

"Older records are kept there."

The Archive Hall

Bill followed her down the corridor.

The air grew cooler as they walked.

The lighting dimmed slightly as well, designed to protect the older materials stored there.

The Archive Hall was quieter than the main chamber.

Shelves rose nearly to the ceiling, filled with preserved documents sealed in protective cases.

Some were written on thin sheets of treated fiber.

Others existed as crystalline data plates.

"These records are rarely used," Tarin explained.

"But they are important."

Bill nodded slowly.

He could feel it already.

This room carried a different kind of quiet.

A deeper quiet.

The quiet of long memory.

An Unusual Container

While organizing a group of storage containers near the back wall, Bill noticed something unusual.

One container looked different from the others.

Its surface was smooth and metallic.

Not Cyrion stonewood.

Not the alloys used in local tools.

Bill knelt beside it.

The material felt strangely familiar.

Along one side were markings he had never seen before.

Symbols.

Carefully etched.

Something about them stirred a strange feeling in his mind.

As if he had seen them somewhere long ago.

But the memory remained just beyond reach.

The Language of Earth

Bill carried the container to one of the reading tables.

Inside were several thin data plates.

When he activated the display surface, the symbols illuminated across the screen.

Bill leaned closer.

His breath caught.

The language was not Cyrion.

Yet somehow he could still understand parts of it.

His enhanced mind recognized the patterns almost immediately.

The shapes of the letters.

The structure of the words.

It was **English**.

The language of **Earth**.

The Ship's Records

The data plates contained records from the crashed ship.

Personal journals.

Navigation logs.

Engineering reports.

Bill read the first entry slowly.

The words described a **colony vessel** traveling toward a distant settlement world.

Passengers.

Families.

Scientists.

Children.

A future waiting somewhere among the stars.

Bill felt his chest tighten.

For the first time he understood something that had always remained hidden from him.

These people…

had been his people.

The Passenger List

One entry included a list of passengers.

Bill scrolled slowly through the names.

Each line described someone who had once lived.

Someone who had boarded the ship with hope.

Then he saw it.

Arden, William II

Age: 1 year.

The words seemed to glow on the screen.

Bill sat motionless.

His hands rested on the edge of the table.

For several minutes he did not move.

Memories returned slowly.

Fragments.

Images.

The faint feeling of being held.

Voices he could almost remember.

Warm light.

Movement.

Then darkness.

He realized something then.

The ship had not simply brought strangers to Cyrion.

It had brought **him**.

A Quiet Decision

Later that evening Bill walked home slowly through the streets of Valaryn.

The sun was setting behind the western ridges.

The **Lumar Plains** had begun their nightly glow.

Dr. Ziv was tending the garden when Bill arrived.

"You were at the library longer than usual," Ziv said.

Bill nodded.

"Yes."

"Did you learn something interesting?"

Bill looked toward the glowing horizon.

He considered telling Ziv everything he had discovered.

But the words did not come easily.

Some discoveries required time to understand.

"Yes," Bill said quietly.

"I did."

Ziv studied him for a moment.

Then he nodded.

He did not press further.

Closing Image

That night Bill sat beside the garden wall with **Ruun** resting quietly nearby.

Above them the **Sky River** stretched across the dark sky.

For many years Bill had wondered where he truly belonged.

Now he knew the answer.

He had come from somewhere far away.

From another world.

Yet as he looked around the quiet valley of Valaryn, another truth felt just as clear.

Cyrion was no longer a place where he had simply survived.

It had become his home.

Interlude — The Search for *Horizon Dawn*

The offices of the **Interstellar Navigation Authority** overlooked the eastern shoreline of Earth's Atlantic continent.

From the wide glass windows, the ocean stretched toward the horizon in deep shades of blue. Cargo vessels moved slowly across the water below while orbital transports rose and descended through the distant sky.

Inside the quiet conference chamber, the atmosphere felt very different.

A long search had reached its final moment.

Twenty Years

The disappearance of the colony vessel **CSV *Horizon Dawn*** had been one of the great mysteries of early expansion.

The ship had departed Earth twenty years earlier with thirty settlers bound for the distant colony world **Hope**.

It had never arrived.

No distress signal had ever been received.

No debris field had ever been found.

The ship had simply vanished.

For most officials within the Authority, the investigation had ended long ago.

Ships were lost sometimes.

The galaxy was a large and unforgiving place.

But one man had refused to let the matter rest.

Lord Arden

At the head of the conference table sat **Lord William Arden**.

Age had placed deep lines across his face, and his hair had long since turned white, but his posture remained straight and composed.

Those who knew him understood that quiet determination was one of his defining traits.

The missing ship had carried his son.

And his son's young family.

For twenty years Arden had funded search missions and investigations across several star systems.

Most had returned with nothing.

But he had never stopped.

The Evidence

A holographic star chart hovered above the center of the table.

Several exploration officers studied the display.

One of them pointed toward a small region near the outer edge of human navigation routes.

"This signal pattern was detected two years ago," she said.

"A faint atmospheric disturbance recorded by a survey probe."

She enlarged the region.

"A planet cataloged as **Survey Object X-8472**."

Arden leaned forward slightly.

"What kind of disturbance?"

"Entry heat signatures," she replied.

"Something large passed through the atmosphere approximately twenty years ago."

The room grew quiet.

A Possibility

Commander **Elena Vance** stood near the far end of the table.

She had spent most of her career flying deep survey missions beyond established routes.

"Most probes would ignore something like that," she said.

"But the timing is interesting."

She gestured toward the star chart.

"The coordinates line up closely with the final projected trajectory of *Horizon Dawn.*"

Arden's eyes remained fixed on the display.

"You believe the ship may have crashed there."

Vance nodded.

"It is possible."

One Final Mission

One of the Authority directors folded his hands.

"**X-8472** is a difficult world," he said.

"High gravity. Dense atmosphere."

"That explains why no distress signal escaped," Vance replied.

The director turned toward Lord Arden.

"This would be a long expedition."

Arden's answer came without hesitation.

"Then we should begin immediately."

The Ship

Three days later the exploration vessel **ISV** ***Aurora Pathfinder*** prepared for departure from Earth's orbital dock.

The ship was not large by colony standards, but it was well suited for deep reconnaissance missions.

Its crew consisted of scientists, pilots, and atmospheric specialists accustomed to difficult environments.

Commander Vance stood on the bridge reviewing the final navigation calculations.

"Course set for Cyrion," the navigator reported.

Estimated travel time: nine weeks.

A Private Moment

Before departure, Arden requested a brief private communication with the commander.

The connection appeared on Vance's console.

The old man's face filled the screen.

"I appreciate your willingness to undertake this mission," he said.

Vance nodded respectfully.

"I believe the evidence deserves investigation."

Arden studied her carefully.

"If the ship did reach that world…"

He paused.

"…someone may still need help."

Vance did not argue.

The Launch

Moments later the **Aurora Pathfinder** disengaged from the orbital dock.

Its engines ignited with a steady blue glow.

The vessel moved slowly away from Earth before turning toward the dark expanse of deep space.

Stars filled the forward viewing screens.

Vance watched them carefully.

"Set course," she said.

The navigator confirmed the coordinates.

"Destination: **X-8472**."

Closing Image

Far behind them, the blue curve of Earth slowly faded into the distance.

Ahead lay a remote world few humans had ever seen.

Somewhere on that distant planet rested the broken remains of a lost colony ship.

And perhaps—if the search had not been in vain—

the final survivor of the **Horizon Dawn**.

Chapter 12 — The Strength of the Body

By the time Bill reached his **sixteenth year**, the people of Valaryn had grown accustomed to seeing him everywhere.

In the mornings he often worked in **Lyara's garden**, tending the rows of blueleaf plants beside **Dr. Arel Ziv**. The irrigation channels that ran through the garden required constant care, and Bill had learned how to adjust the flow of water with steady hands.

By midday he might be found in the **Library of Valaryn**, carrying stacks of books between the reading tables or organizing the archive shelves deep within the stone chambers.

In the afternoons he sometimes helped at the small **market hall**, unloading supply carts or arranging produce brought in from the farms beyond the valley.

It had taken many years for his body to reach that point.

But it had happened.

Slowly.

The Change

Cyrion's gravity shaped everything that lived on the planet.

Plants grew thick and strong.

Animals developed dense muscle and powerful limbs.

Even the people of the valley carried themselves with a natural strength that came from generations of life under the heavy sky.

For Bill, that strength had not come naturally.

It had come through effort.

Every day since childhood he had pushed himself to walk farther, climb higher, and work longer.

There had been many mornings when his muscles ached so badly he wondered if he would ever truly belong to this world.

But each day he tried again.

At first the tasks had seemed impossible.

Now they were simply part of life.

A Morning in the Garden

One morning Ziv watched Bill lifting a heavy irrigation stone that had shifted during the previous night's rain.

Water had begun to spill past the edge of the channel and into one of the garden beds.

Bill knelt beside the stone and studied the problem carefully.

Then he placed both hands beneath the rough edge and lifted.

The stone was large—far larger than the kind Bill would once have struggled even to move.

Now he shifted it slowly, guiding it back into position so the channel walls fit together again.

The water settled into its proper path.

Ziv folded his arms thoughtfully.

"You have grown stronger," he said.

Bill wiped the dirt from his hands.

"I've had a lot of practice."

Ziv smiled.

"That you have."

The Market Hall

Later that week Bill was helping unload produce at the market.

Large crates of **tallroot vegetables** had arrived from a farm several miles outside the valley.

Two Cyrion farmers struggled briefly to maneuver one of the heavier containers from their cart.

Bill stepped forward.

"Here," he said.

He lifted one side of the crate while the farmers lifted the other.

Together they carried it easily into the storage room.

The farmers exchanged surprised glances.

One of them laughed.

"Well," he said, "the human is finally learning how to work."

Bill shrugged.

"What else is one to do?"

The farmer chuckled again.

"Fair answer."

The Path to the Stone Forest

In the evenings Bill often walked the ridge path beyond Valaryn with **Ruun** trotting beside him.

The path eventually led toward the towering formations of the **Talen Stone Forest**, where wind carved strange shapes into the massive pillars of rock.

The pillars rose hundreds of feet into the air.

Their surfaces were rough and uneven, marked with natural ledges and narrow crevices.

Climbing there had once seemed impossible.

Now Bill practiced on the lower formations, testing his strength and balance against the stone.

Each climb demanded careful planning.

Each movement required steady control beneath the heavy gravity of Cyrion.

Sometimes he reached the top of a pillar.

Sometimes he slipped and had to begin again.

Each climb taught him something new.

Each fall taught him something as well.

Ziv's Observation

One evening Ziv joined him near the base of one of the stone pillars.

Bill had just finished a difficult climb, pulling himself onto a narrow ledge several meters above the ground.

When he reached the top he sat there catching his breath.

The wind moved through the high stone formations, carrying cool air down into the valley.

Ziv looked up from below.

"You move more naturally now," he said.

Bill climbed down carefully.

"I still move slower than everyone else."

Ziv nodded.

"That may always be true."

Bill considered that.

"But you no longer struggle against the world," Ziv continued.

"You move with it."

Bill looked back toward the towering stone pillars.

He had not thought about it that way.

But perhaps it was true.

The world no longer felt like an obstacle.

It felt like something he had learned to understand.

The Town Notices

Over time the people of Valaryn began noticing the change.

The once-fragile boy who had needed help simply to walk across the garden path was now working alongside farmers and laborers.

He did not boast about his strength.

He rarely even mentioned it.

But when a task needed doing, Bill quietly stepped forward.

A broken irrigation gate.

A fallen cart wheel.

A heavy crate that needed lifting.

And somehow, the task always seemed to get done.

The people of the valley began to trust that quiet reliability.

A Quiet Respect

One evening as Bill and Ziv walked through the town square, an older craftsman paused beside them.

The man carried a bundle of carved tools beneath one arm.

"I remember when the boy first came here," the craftsman said.

Ziv nodded.

"So do I."

The craftsman looked at Bill thoughtfully.

"You were very small then."

Bill smiled slightly.

"I remember."

The craftsman gestured toward the **Stone Forest** rising in the distance.

"You climb there now, don't you?"

Bill nodded.

"Yes."

The craftsman studied him for a moment longer.

Then he gave a short approving nod and continued on his way.

It was a small gesture.

But in Valaryn, small gestures often carried great meaning.

Closing Image

Later that night Bill stood at the edge of the ridge above Valaryn.

The **Lumar Plains** glowed softly beneath the rising moons.

Ruun rested beside him, watching the quiet valley below.

Bill stretched his arms slowly, feeling the strength in his muscles.

For the first time he could remember, Cyrion's gravity no longer felt like an enemy.

It felt like part of him.

The world had shaped him.

And he had grown strong enough to shape himself in return.

Chapter 13 — The First Rescue

Late summer had come to the valley of Valaryn.

The air was warm, and the winds moving through the **Stone Forest** carried the dry scent of distant plains. Farmers were busy gathering the season's final crops, and the town's **market hall** remained crowded throughout the day.

Carts rolled through the central square carrying baskets of tallroot vegetables and bundles of drying grain. Voices echoed between the stone pillars as merchants arranged their tables and buyers moved between the stalls.

Bill spent the morning in the **Library of Valaryn**, returning several storage tablets to the archive shelves.

The work required careful attention.

Some of the older records were fragile, and the librarians trusted Bill to handle them properly.

When the last tablet was returned to its place, he stepped outside into the bright sunlight.

Ruun was waiting near the library steps.

The young Varik's tail swayed slowly as he watched the movement of people across the square.

"Come on," Bill said, scratching behind the animal's ear.

Ruun stood immediately.

The two of them headed toward the ridge path that led into the hills beyond the town.

The Path Above the Valley

The trail wound upward through low grasses and scattered stone formations.

From the higher slopes the entire valley of Valaryn could be seen stretching below, with fields and gardens surrounding the town's buildings.

The irrigation channels glimmered faintly in the sunlight.

Beyond them the glowing plains of Cyrion stretched toward the distant horizon.

Bill liked walking there.

The quiet helped him think.

He had spent much of the previous night reading the ship logs in the library, learning more about the world he had come from.

The knowledge still felt strange.

Earth.

Another planet.

Another life he had never known.

Sometimes he wondered what those passengers had hoped to find when they began their journey through the stars.

Ruun trotted ahead of him along the trail, pausing occasionally to sniff the wind.

The Cry

Halfway along the ridge trail, Bill heard something.

A voice.

Faint.

He stopped immediately.

Ruun's ears lifted.

The sound came again.

"Help!"

Bill turned toward the cliffs that rose along the northern edge of the trail.

Someone was calling from above.

The Cliff

Bill ran toward the base of the cliff.

The rock face rose sharply from the hillside, forming a steep wall of broken ledges and narrow handholds.

Far above, a small figure clung to the stone.

It was **Lina**, one of the younger students from the Learning Hall.

She had been exploring the lower ledges of the ridge.

Now she was trapped.

Loose stones had collapsed beneath her feet, leaving her stranded on a narrow shelf.

The drop below her was steep enough to cause serious injury.

Bill studied the rock face carefully.

Years of climbing in the **Talen Stone Forest** had taught him how to read the patterns of the stone.

He could see the path immediately.

The Ascent

"Stay where you are!" he called.

"I'm coming."

Lina looked down, frightened.

Her hands clung tightly to the rough rock.

Bill placed his hands on the first ledge and began climbing.

Each movement had to be precise.

Cyrion's gravity made every pull heavier than it would have been on Earth.

But his muscles were strong now—shaped by years of climbing and work.

Handhold.

Step.

Pull.

Handhold.

Step.

Pull.

Below him Ruun paced anxiously along the base of the cliff.

The Varik's eyes never left the climbers above.

The Slip

Halfway up the wall a section of rock broke loose beneath Bill's foot.

The stone tumbled down the cliff, striking the ground below with a sharp crack.

For a moment Bill hung by one arm.

The weight of the planet pulled hard against his shoulder.

But his other hand quickly found the next hold.

He tightened his grip and pulled himself upward again.

Above him Lina watched in silence.

She did not dare move.

The Rescue

Within minutes Bill reached the narrow shelf where she stood.

The girl's face was pale.

Her breathing came in short frightened bursts.

"I can't climb down," she whispered.

Bill glanced at the broken stones beneath her.

"You don't have to."

He positioned himself carefully beside her.

The ledge was barely wide enough for both of them.

"Hold on to my shoulders," he said.

She hesitated only a moment.

Then she did exactly as he said.

Her arms wrapped tightly around him.

The Descent

Climbing down was harder.

Bill moved slowly, keeping one arm steady around Lina while his other hand searched for secure holds.

The weight of two people pressed heavily against his muscles.

Every step had to be perfect.

Below them Ruun watched every movement, pacing back and forth across the ground.

Several minutes passed.

Then Bill reached the final ledge.

One more careful step.

His feet touched the ground.

The Crowd

Lina stepped away from him, still trembling.

"Thank you," she said quietly.

Bill brushed dust from his hands.

"You're welcome."

By then several townspeople had arrived, drawn by the earlier cries for help.

A small crowd gathered near the base of the cliff.

One of the elders approached slowly.

"You climbed that wall carrying her?" he asked.

Bill shrugged slightly.

"It seemed like the fastest way."

The elder looked up at the steep rock face again.

The climb was difficult even for strong adults.

Then he nodded.

A Quiet Beginning

As the crowd slowly dispersed, Lina's parents hurried forward.

They thanked Bill repeatedly, relief clear on their faces.

Bill accepted their gratitude with quiet embarrassment.

Later, as he and Ruun walked back toward Valaryn, Bill said nothing about the rescue.

To him it had seemed obvious.

Someone needed help.

So he helped them.

Closing Image

That evening the sun set slowly over the valley.

Bill stood beside **Dr. Arel Ziv** in the garden.

"I heard about the climb today," Ziv said.

Bill looked slightly uncomfortable.

"She was stuck."

Ziv nodded thoughtfully.

"Yes."

He studied the young man for a moment.

"You did not climb for praise."

Bill shook his head.

"No."

Ziv smiled.

"That is why people will remember it."

Bill looked out across the glowing valley.

He did not yet realize it.

But the people of Valaryn had begun to see something new in him.

Not simply strength.

Not simply intelligence.

Something deeper.

The heart of a protector.

Chapter 14 — The Night Alone

Among the traditions of Valaryn, there was one that every young person eventually faced.

It was not written into law.

It was not announced with ceremony.

Yet everyone understood it.

At some point, before entering adulthood, a person would spend **one night alone in the wilderness of Cyrion**.

The tradition had begun long before the town itself existed. The earliest settlers of the valley believed that no person could truly understand life until they had listened to the quiet of the world itself.

Not the voices of neighbors.

Not the instruction of teachers.

Only the wind, the land, and their own thoughts.

The purpose was simple.

To listen.

To think.

And to understand one's place in the world.

The Decision

Bill chose his night in **early autumn**.

The valley had grown cooler, and the winds moving across the distant plains carried the dry scent of stone and sun-warmed grasses.

That evening he stood in **Lyara's garden** beside **Dr. Arel Ziv**.

The sun was lowering toward the western ridges, and long shadows stretched across the rows of blueleaf plants.

"I am going to the ridge tonight," Bill said.

Ziv looked at him quietly.

"You have thought about this?"

"Yes."

Ziv studied his face for a moment.

Then he nodded.

"Then it is time."

Bill gathered a small pack containing water, a blanket, and a simple lantern.

Nothing more.

The tradition required little.

Understanding rarely came from equipment.

As Bill stepped toward the gate, **Ruun** rose from his resting place beside the garden wall.

The Varik followed him immediately.

Bill stopped and knelt beside the animal.

"Not tonight."

Ruun tilted his head.

Bill scratched behind the animal's ear.

"This is something I must do alone."

Ruun looked disappointed, but after a moment the Varik lay back down beside the garden wall.

Leaving the Valley

The path leading out of Valaryn wound upward toward the high ridges overlooking the valley.

Bill walked slowly.

The air cooled as he climbed.

Cyrion's gravity pressed steadily against his body, a familiar weight that he had learned to live with over many years.

Once it had felt like an enemy.

Now it felt almost comforting.

A reminder that he belonged to this place.

Behind him the lights of Valaryn began to appear.

Small golden points scattered among the stone buildings.

Soon the sounds of the town faded completely.

Only the wind remained.

The Ridge

Bill reached the overlook just as the final light of sunset disappeared behind the western cliffs.

From that height he could see nearly the entire valley.

The farms.

The irrigation channels.

The gardens surrounding the town.

Beyond them stretched the faint blue glow of the **Lumar Plains**, already beginning their nightly illumination.

The glowing moss spread across the distant landscape like a silent sea of light.

Bill sat on a flat stone near the edge of the ridge.

Night settled slowly around him.

The Sky

Above him the stars began to appear.

First a few.

Then dozens.

Then hundreds.

Soon the bright band of the **Sky River** stretched across the heavens like a glowing road between worlds.

Bill lay back against the cool stone and watched them.

Somewhere among those distant lights was the world where he had been born.

Earth.

The ship logs in the library had told him that much.

But the idea still felt strange.

Distant.

Almost unreal.

Like a story belonging to someone else.

Two Worlds

Bill closed his eyes for a moment.

His earliest memories belonged entirely to Cyrion.

The garden.

The valley.

Dr. Ziv.

The Stone Forest.

The quiet evenings beneath the twin moons.

Even the heavy gravity that shaped every movement of his body.

Everything that mattered to him had grown from this world.

Yet the records in the library had revealed another truth.

He had not begun here.

He had arrived.

Carried across the stars in a ship he could barely remember.

Bill opened his eyes again.

Two worlds.

One he had never known.

And one that had raised him.

The Quiet

The wind moved gently across the ridge.

Far below, a faint glow marked the edge of Valaryn.

Bill listened to the silence.

For the first time in his life, there were no voices nearby.

No footsteps.

No sound of Ruun breathing beside him.

Only the quiet presence of the planet itself.

Cyrion felt enormous.

Older than anything he could imagine.

Yet somehow it did not feel distant.

It felt welcoming.

Ziv's Words

Bill remembered something Ziv had once told him.

"Where you begin does not decide who you become."

At the time the words had seemed simple.

Now they carried greater weight.

Bill looked toward the glowing plains again.

Cyrion had not been the world of his birth.

But it had become the world of his life.

The world that had shaped his body.

And his heart.

The Night Watchers

As the hours passed, the wilderness around him slowly revealed itself.

Large birdlike creatures glided across the sky, their wide wings catching the faint light of the moons.

Somewhere below, a small animal moved through the grasses.

The night insects began their soft rhythmic sounds.

The wilderness of Cyrion was alive even in the deepest darkness.

Bill felt no fear.

Instead he felt something else.

A deep calm.

Peace.

Dawn

Eventually the eastern sky began to lighten.

The stars faded one by one.

The Sky River slowly dissolved into the pale blue of early morning.

A thin line of sunlight appeared beyond the distant mountains.

Bill stood slowly.

He had not slept.

Yet he did not feel tired.

He felt clear.

Certain.

Closing Image

When Bill returned to **Lyara's garden**, Dr. Arel Ziv was already working among the rows of blueleaf plants.

The morning sun cast long golden light across the valley.

Ziv looked up.

"You stayed the night."

"Yes."

Ziv studied him carefully.

"Did you learn anything?"

Bill considered the question for a moment.

Then he nodded.

"Yes."

"And what did you learn?"

Bill looked across the valley toward the rising sun.

"That this world is not where I began."

Ziv waited.

"But it is where I belong."

Ziv smiled quietly.

"That is a very good thing to discover."

The morning wind moved gently through the garden.

And for the first time in many years, Bill felt completely certain of who he was becoming.

Chapter 15 — The Name of Endurance

Autumn settled gently over the valley of **Valaryn**.

The winds moving through the **Stone Forest** carried cooler air now, and the leaves of the tallroot vines in **Lyara's garden** had begun to darken toward deep shades of blue and purple.

The harvest season had nearly ended.

Farmers moved steadily through the surrounding fields gathering the final crops before the colder winds arrived from the northern plains.

Bill had grown into a young man.

His shoulders had broadened, his hands had grown strong from years of work, and the careful patience he had learned as a child had settled naturally into his movements.

Where once he had struggled simply to walk beneath Cyrion's gravity, he now climbed the high ridges above the valley with steady confidence.

The people of Valaryn noticed.

But Bill himself thought very little about it.

To him, work was simply part of life.

The Work of the Town

One morning the townspeople gathered along the **northern irrigation channel** that carried water from the mountain streams into the farms surrounding the valley.

During the previous night's winds, part of the stone barrier controlling the water flow had collapsed.

If the channel remained open, too much water would rush through the lower fields and flood the crops.

Farmers had arrived quickly to repair the damage.

Several workers were already clearing the broken stones when Bill arrived along the path.

He paused briefly to study the problem.

Then he stepped into the work without a word.

No one asked him to help.

But no one was surprised to see him there either.

The Problem

As the workers cleared the smaller rocks, the real difficulty became clear.

One massive **stone slab** had fallen sideways into the water flow.

The slab was ancient.

It had been part of the irrigation structure for decades.

Now it lay wedged in the channel like a door stuck halfway open.

Water rushed violently around its edges, spilling into the surrounding soil.

If the stone remained where it was, the entire wall might collapse.

Two strong farmers pushed against the slab.

The stone barely moved.

Another joined them.

Still nothing.

The water continued to surge through the opening.

A Different Approach

Bill stood quietly for several moments, watching the movement of the water.

He studied the angle of the slab.

The pressure of the current.

The balance of the surrounding stones.

Years of climbing and labor had taught him something important:

Strength alone was rarely enough.

Understanding mattered just as much.

He stepped into the shallow water.

"Wait," he said.

The workers paused.

Bill placed his hands against the stone.

"Push when I say."

The men looked at one another but nodded.

Bill watched the current carefully.

The water surged in rhythmic waves through the broken section.

He waited for the moment when the pressure would shift.

Then he braced himself.

"Now."

The Lift

The workers pushed together.

The stone shifted slightly.

Water splashed around their legs as the current fought against the movement.

Bill adjusted his footing against the riverbed.

Cyrion's gravity pressed heavily against his muscles.

But the years of climbing and lifting had prepared him for exactly this kind of effort.

"Again," he said.

The men pushed harder.

The slab lifted higher.

Water rushed beneath it.

Bill pulled upward with every bit of strength he had.

The muscles in his arms and shoulders strained beneath the weight.

Slowly—inch by inch—the stone rotated.

Then it dropped back into its original position against the channel wall.

The water flow changed instantly.

The current settled into the proper channel once again.

The Silence

For a moment no one spoke.

The workers stepped back and studied the repaired wall.

Water flowed smoothly through the irrigation channel as if nothing had happened.

An older farmer shook his head slowly.

"That stone has not moved in thirty years," he said.

Bill stepped out of the water and wiped the mud from his hands.

"It just needed a better angle."

Several of the workers exchanged quiet smiles.

The Elder's Words

Later that afternoon several elders gathered near the **town square.**

One of them had watched the entire event from the nearby ridge.

"That boy has done something like this before," the elder said.

"Yes," another replied.

"He climbs where others cannot."

"He lifts when others struggle."

"And he does not boast about it."

The first elder nodded slowly.

"Strength is common on Cyrion."

He looked toward the distant hills.

"But **endurance** is rarer."

The Name

That evening many of the townspeople gathered in the square as the sun dipped behind the western ridges.

The gathering was informal, but the mood carried quiet importance.

Bill arrived without realizing anything unusual was happening.

He had come only to return a tool to the workshop.

One of the elders stepped forward.

"You were not born on Cyrion," the elder said.

Bill nodded.

"That is true."

"But you have lived as one of us."

The elder turned and looked across the gathered crowd.

"You endure what others avoid."

"You help when help is needed."

"And you do these things without seeking reward."

The elder paused.

"In our language there is a word for such a person."

Bill listened quietly.

The elder spoke the word clearly.

"Torlan Tarsen."

A quiet murmur moved through the crowd.

The word carried meaning older than the town itself.

It meant:

Torlan — Enduring traveler / one who walks the long path.

Tarsen — son of strength / bearer of strength.

Acceptance

Bill looked around the square.

He saw farmers he had worked beside in the fields.

Children who had once laughed at his slow steps.

Scholars from the library.

And **Dr. Arel Ziv**, standing quietly near the back.

Ziv gave a small approving nod.

Bill turned back toward the elder.

"If that is the name you wish to use," he said calmly,

"then I will accept it."

The elder smiled.

"It is the name you have earned."

Closing Image

Later that night Bill stood beside the ridge overlooking the valley.

Beside him sat **Ruun**, watching the distant glow of the **Lumar Plains**.

Behind him, the lights of Valaryn shone warmly against the dark landscape.

For the first time in his life, the people of Cyrion had given him a name that belonged entirely to this world.

Torlan Tarsen.

Bill tested the sound quietly in his mind.

It felt right.

And somewhere in the quiet valley below, the people of Valaryn had begun telling a new story.

The story of the human who had become one of them.

Chapter 16 — The Storm That Changed Valaryn

The first warning came in the wind.

For several days the air across the valley of **Valaryn** had carried an unusual heaviness. The breezes that normally drifted gently through the **Stone Forest** now arrived in uneven bursts, pushing against the tall grasses and bending the tops of the ancient stone pillars.

Birds that usually circled the valley flew lower than usual.

Even the small grazing animals that wandered the outer fields seemed restless.

Dr. **Arel Ziv** noticed it immediately.

He stood outside the house one morning, studying the western sky.

The clouds there were darker than usual.

Much darker.

They formed a long rising wall along the horizon.

Ziv had seen many storms in his lifetime.

But something about this one troubled him.

The Instruments

Inside the laboratory, Ziv checked the atmospheric monitors.

The instruments glowed softly as they processed the incoming data.

Pressure levels were dropping faster than normal.

Electrical readings in the upper atmosphere were rising.

Wind shear patterns stretched across hundreds of kilometers.

Ziv leaned closer to the display.

This was no ordinary **Storm Wall.**

The system forming beyond the western ridges was enormous.

Ziv frowned.

Then he called out toward the garden.

"**Torlan.**"

Bill stepped inside.

"Yes?"

Ziv gestured toward the display.

"Look."

Torlan studied the data carefully.

Years earlier he might have struggled to understand the readings.

Now his enhanced mind processed the information quickly.

The storm forming beyond the western ridges was massive.

Larger than any recorded in the recent weather archives.

"How long?" he asked.

"Perhaps twelve hours," Ziv replied.

Torlan nodded slowly.

"That is not much time."

The Warning

Word spread quickly through Valaryn.

The town had faced many storms before, and the people knew what to do.

Farmers secured equipment.

Workers reinforced irrigation gates.

Market stalls were closed early.

Families sealed windows and prepared the underground storm shelters built beneath many of the buildings.

Yet as Torlan walked along the northern ridge, one concern stayed in his mind.

The **northern wind barriers**.

Those structures had protected Valaryn for generations.

Long stone walls and heavy wooden braces redirected the worst of the storm winds around the valley.

But several sections had weakened over the years.

Under normal storms they held.

This storm would be different.

The Plan

Torlan gathered several workers near the base of the ridge.

Dark clouds were already rising above the distant plains.

"If the barrier fails," he explained, "the wind will strike the town directly."

The workers studied the approaching sky.

"What can we do?" one asked.

Torlan examined the structure carefully.

The central supports were the weakest point.

If they failed, the entire barrier would collapse.

"We reinforce the center supports," he said.

"With what?" another worker asked.

Torlan pointed toward the nearby stone quarry.

"Those."

The Work

For the next several hours the town worked together.

Teams hauled heavy stone braces and thick support beams toward the wind barrier.

The work was exhausting.

Cyrion's gravity made every lift harder.

But the people of Valaryn were used to difficult labor.

Torlan moved constantly along the barrier.

He directed the placement of the reinforcements with calm precision.

"Move that brace two meters left."

"Secure the beam against the lower joint."

"The wind will strike here first."

His understanding of the storm patterns allowed him to predict where the pressure would be greatest.

Several workers paused to rest.

Torlan did not.

He continued helping lift beams into place beside them.

Throughout the work, **Ruun** remained close by, watching the darkening sky with alert eyes.

The Arrival

The Storm Wall reached the valley just after nightfall.

From the northern ridge it appeared like a moving mountain of cloud and lightning.

The wind struck the outer ridges first.

A deep roar rolled across the valley.

Moments later the full force of the storm arrived.

Wind slammed against the barrier with tremendous power.

The reinforced structure groaned under the pressure.

Rain slashed across the hillside.

Lightning illuminated the sky again and again, revealing the vast rolling wall of clouds overhead.

Torlan stood beside the central support beam.

"Hold the line!" someone shouted.

The Breaking Point

A loud crack echoed through the storm.

One of the outer sections of the barrier splintered.

A wooden support beam snapped beneath the force of the wind.

Torlan saw it instantly.

"If that collapses," he shouted, "the entire section will fall!"

Without hesitation he ran toward the damaged support.

The wind nearly knocked him sideways.

Several workers followed him through the driving rain.

Together they pushed a massive reinforcement stone toward the failing beam.

The wind fought them every step of the way.

For a moment it seemed impossible.

The stone refused to move.

Then Torlan braced himself against the ground and pushed with everything he had.

"Now!"

The workers surged forward.

The stone dropped into place beneath the broken support.

The barrier steadied.

The wind howled against the reinforced wall.

But it held.

The Long Night

The storm raged for hours.

Wind screamed through the valley.

Lightning turned the sky white again and again.

Rain flooded the slopes and rushed through the irrigation channels.

Yet the barrier remained standing.

Slowly, hour by hour, the Storm Wall moved eastward.

Eventually the wind weakened.

The thunder faded.

And the storm passed across the glowing plains of Cyrion.

After the Storm

Morning revealed the damage.

Several trees had fallen across the outer fields.

A few storage sheds had collapsed beneath the wind.

But the town itself remained standing.

Farmers walked the irrigation channels inspecting the fields.

Children emerged cautiously from the storm shelters.

The people of Valaryn gathered near the northern ridge.

The reinforced barrier still stood.

The Recognition

Later that day the elders gathered beside the structure.

Many people had worked through the storm.

But everyone understood who had seen the danger first.

And who had guided the work that saved the town.

The elder who had spoken the name **Torlan Tarsen** months earlier stepped forward.

"You did not command the storm," the elder said.

Torlan shook his head.

"No."

"But you helped the town endure it."

The elder looked toward the barrier.

"That is what the name means."

Closing Image

That evening Torlan stood once again on the ridge above Valaryn.

The storm clouds had cleared.

The **Sky River** stretched across the stars.

Beside him, **Dr. Arel Ziv** watched the quiet valley below.

"You saw the problem before anyone else," Ziv said.

Torlan shrugged.

"The signs were there."

Ziv smiled.

"They were."

Torlan looked across the town he had helped protect.

The lights of Valaryn shone warmly against the dark plains.

For the first time he realized something fully.

This world had not only shaped him.

He had begun to shape it in return.

Chapter 17 — The Weight of Two Worlds

The valley of **Valaryn** slowly returned to its ordinary rhythm after the great storm.

Broken trees were cleared from the roads. Farmers repaired damaged irrigation channels. The wind barriers along the northern ridge were strengthened even further, their foundations now reinforced with stone that would likely endure for generations.

Life on **Cyrion** always moved forward.

The planet had little patience for those who wished to linger in the past.

Storms passed.

Fields were repaired.

Work resumed.

Yet for **Torlan Tarsen**, the days following the storm brought a different kind of quiet.

The town now spoke his name with a new kind of respect.

Where once he had been the boy who struggled beneath Cyrion's gravity, he had become the young man who had helped the town endure its greatest storm.

Torlan accepted the change calmly.

But inside his thoughts had begun turning toward something deeper.

The Library Again

One afternoon Torlan returned to the **Library of Valaryn.**

The building stood silent beneath the afternoon light, its stone pillars casting long shadows across the courtyard.

Inside, the familiar scent of old paper and polished wood filled the air.

The library was nearly empty.

Only the faint rustle of turning pages and the distant tapping of a scholar's stylus disturbed the quiet.

Torlan walked slowly toward the archive room.

He had not visited the ship logs for several weeks.

But something had drawn him back.

Perhaps it was the storm.

Perhaps it was the way the people of Valaryn now looked at him.

Or perhaps it was the quiet realization that his life had begun somewhere far beyond the sky above this valley.

The Old Records

The storage container holding the logs from the crashed ship still rested on the archive table where he had last studied it.

Torlan opened the container and activated the display.

Soft light filled the screen.

The familiar English text appeared again.

Passenger manifests.

Engineering reports.

Navigation logs.

Personal journals.

Each entry was a small window into a life that had ended long ago.

Lives that had once traveled across the stars with hope for a new world.

Torlan read slowly.

His mind absorbed every detail.

His Parents

One journal entry belonged to a woman named **Elena Arden**.

Torlan had read portions of it before.

But this time he read the entries more carefully.

Elena wrote about the long journey aboard the colony vessel **CSV Horizon Dawn**.

She described the artificial daylight cycles inside the ship.

The quiet hum of the engines that pushed the vessel through deep space.

The excitement of the passengers who believed they were traveling toward a new beginning.

And often she wrote about the child traveling with her.

A small boy.

Her son.

Torlan paused.

The words on the screen felt strangely personal.

The child she described could only be one person.

Him.

A Life Never Known

Torlan leaned back slowly in the chair.

He tried to imagine the ship as it had once been.

Families walking the wide corridors.

Children playing beneath the glow of artificial lights.

Passengers gathering near the viewing decks to watch the endless fields of stars drifting past the windows.

Somewhere within that world, a young mother had held her child and dreamed about the future.

A future waiting on a distant planet called **Hope**.

But the ship had never reached that world.

Something had gone wrong.

The vessel had fallen from the sky.

And the future those passengers had imagined had ended in the wilderness of Cyrion.

Ziv's Question

Later that evening Torlan returned to **Lyara's garden**.

Dr. **Arel Ziv** was trimming the tallroot vines along the stone wall.

The scent of the garden filled the cool evening air.

"You went to the library again," Ziv said without looking up.

"Yes."

Ziv studied him for a moment.

"Reading the ship logs?"

Torlan nodded.

The Question of Belonging

They sat together on the familiar stone bench.

The garden was quiet.

The wind moved softly through the leaves above them.

For a long time neither spoke.

Finally Ziv said quietly,

"You are thinking about where you belong."

Torlan did not deny it.

"I was born somewhere else," he said.

"Yes."

"But I don't remember it."

Ziv folded his hands calmly.

"Memory is only one way of belonging."

Two Truths

Torlan looked toward the darkening valley.

Lights had begun appearing in the windows of the houses below.

"Sometimes I wonder what my life would have been like if the ship had never crashed."

Ziv followed his gaze.

"You might have grown up on another world."

"Yes."

Torlan paused.

"But then I would never have known this one."

Ziv smiled faintly.

"That is also true."

The Balance

The first stars appeared overhead.

The bright band of the **Sky River** slowly stretched across the heavens.

Ziv pointed upward.

"Somewhere among those stars is the world where you began."

Torlan looked up at the sky.

A vast ocean of light filled the darkness above them.

"And here is the world where you grew."

Ziv gestured toward the valley below.

The farms.

The town.

The quiet lights of Valaryn.

Both statements were true.

And both carried weight.

The Answer

Torlan thought about it for a long time.

Finally he spoke.

"I think a person can belong to more than one world."

Ziv nodded.

"Yes."

Torlan rested his hands on the stone bench.

"But the world that teaches you how to live…"

He looked across the quiet valley.

"…that one stays with you."

Ziv smiled.

"That is wisdom."

Closing Image

Night deepened over Cyrion.

Torlan remained seated in **Lyara's garden**, watching the distant glow of the **Lumar Plains**.

Two worlds now existed in his story.

One written in the ship logs preserved in the library.

And one alive around him in the valley that had raised him.

The weight of those two worlds no longer felt like a burden.

It felt like a responsibility.

And though Torlan could not yet know it, the stars above him were already carrying a new visitor toward Cyrion.

Someone who had been searching for the lost ship **Horizon Dawn** for many years.

Chapter 18 — The Signal in the Sky

The evening began like many others in the valley of **Valaryn**.

The day's work had ended, and the town had settled into its quiet evening rhythm. Lamps glowed in the windows of the stone houses, and the soft blue light of the **Lumar Plains** shimmered across the distant horizon.

The smell of cooking fires drifted through the streets.

Children's voices echoed faintly from the courtyard near the **Learning Hall** before fading as families returned indoors for the night.

In **Lyara's garden**, Torlan helped **Dr. Arel Ziv** harvest the last of the tallroot vegetables before the cooler nights of late autumn arrived.

The soil was still warm from the afternoon sun.

The wind moved gently through the vines.

Everything felt calm.

Everything felt ordinary.

Then the sky changed.

The First Light

At first it was only a faint streak above the western horizon.

So faint that it might have been mistaken for a falling star.

Torlan noticed it before Ziv did.

He straightened slowly and looked toward the darkening sky.

"That one is moving," he said.

Ziv glanced up.

Most stars remained fixed in their slow celestial paths.

But one bright point of light was traveling steadily across the sky.

Not falling.

Not drifting.

Moving with clear direction.

Ziv's expression changed immediately.

"That is no star."

The Town Notices

Within minutes the unusual light had drawn the attention of others in Valaryn.

A woman stepped out of her home and pointed toward the sky.

Two children ran into the street to watch.

Soon small groups gathered throughout the town square.

People shaded their eyes and stared upward.

The object grew brighter as it crossed the heavens.

Occasionally it flashed with brief pulses of light.

Precise flashes.

Regular intervals.

Signals.

Ziv's voice grew quiet.

"That is a spacecraft."

The word spread quickly among the people gathered in the streets.

A ship.

A vessel built by travelers between worlds.

Few in Valaryn had ever seen such a thing.

A Long Silence

For a moment Torlan said nothing.

He simply watched the moving light.

A ship.

Something built by people who traveled between the stars.

Something like the vessel that had once brought him to Cyrion.

For many years he had known such ships existed.

The logs in the library had described them.

The crashed wreckage in the distant valley had proven it.

But knowing something existed was very different from seeing it.

Now one was actually above him.

Crossing the sky of the world he called home.

The Approach

The ship slowed as it entered **Cyrion's upper atmosphere**.

The light surrounding it brightened briefly as the vessel adjusted to the dense air and heavy gravity of the planet.

Several smaller flashes appeared around it as maneuvering thrusters corrected its descent path.

Ziv studied the motion carefully.

His scientist's mind quickly interpreted the patterns.

"They are searching," he said.

"For what?" someone nearby asked.

Ziv looked toward Torlan.

"For the wreck."

The Old Wreck

High above the valley, the ship adjusted its course.

The lights of its engines shifted slightly northward.

Toward the crash site of the **CSV Horizon Dawn**.

Even after all these years, fragments of the colony vessel still lay scattered across the distant valley floor.

Some of the metal sections had been buried by wind and dust.

Others remained exposed, silent reminders of the disaster that had brought Torlan to Cyrion.

Torlan felt a strange tightening in his chest.

Someone out there had come looking.

Looking for the ship.

Looking for the passengers who had vanished so long ago.

Looking for the families who had never arrived at their destination.

A Message

Suddenly a beam of light flashed downward from the spacecraft.

The beam swept slowly across the valley.

Not a weapon.

A scanning signal.

The light passed across the outer farms.

Across the towering formations of the **Stone Forest**.

Across the high ridge where Torlan had once spent his night alone.

Finally the beam swept across Valaryn itself.

For a moment the entire town glowed beneath the pale light.

Then the beam faded.

Moments later the spacecraft transmitted another signal.

A bright sequence of flashes.

Short.

Short.

Long.

Long.

Short.

Ziv watched carefully.

His expression softened.

"It's a greeting code," he said quietly.

"Human."

The Meaning

A murmur spread through the gathered townspeople.

Visitors from another world had arrived above Cyrion.

The idea filled many of them with curiosity.

Some with excitement.

Others with caution.

But Torlan understood something else.

The ship had not come randomly.

It had come searching for the lost colony vessel.

Searching for the passengers who had vanished.

And somehow…

after twenty years…

they had found the right planet.

A Different Kind of Silence

Gradually the crowd dispersed.

People returned to their homes, talking quietly about the strange visitor in the sky.

But Torlan remained standing in the garden beside Ziv.

Above them the spacecraft now hovered far above the valley.

Its lights shone steadily against the dark sky.

"They will come down tomorrow," Ziv said.

Torlan nodded.

"Yes."

Ziv studied him carefully.

"You have been waiting for this moment all your life."

Torlan looked toward the glowing valley.

"I didn't know I was waiting."

Closing Image

Later that night Torlan stood alone on the ridge above Valaryn.

The wind moved softly across the grasses.

Far above him the distant ship glowed among the stars.

For the first time in many years, the path between worlds had opened again.

The people of Earth had finally found the lost ship.

And tomorrow they would discover something they had never expected.

One passenger had survived.

And he had become someone entirely different from the child they had lost.

Chapter 19 — The Visitors from Earth

Morning came early to the valley of **Valaryn**.

Long before the sun reached the tops of the eastern ridges, people were already gathering in the open fields north of the town. Farmers left their tools beside the irrigation channels. Merchants closed the doors of their market stalls. Children hurried along the stone paths, whispering excitedly to one another.

Word had spread quickly during the night.

The visitors from the sky were coming down.

No one in Valaryn wanted to miss the moment.

The Descent

Far above the valley, the spacecraft moved slowly through **Cyrion's atmosphere**.

Its engines glowed with a controlled blue light as the vessel adjusted to the planet's heavy gravity and dense air. Thin lines of vapor formed along the edges of its hull as the ship stabilized its descent.

The people of Valaryn watched in complete silence.

None of them had ever seen such a vessel before.

To them it looked like a small star lowering itself toward the earth.

The ship circled once above the valley, scanning the terrain. Its sensors swept across the surrounding cliffs, the farms, and the distant Stone Forest.

Then the vessel angled downward.

Slowly.

Carefully.

It descended toward the open field beyond the irrigation channels.

With a final burst of light from its maneuvering thrusters, the engines faded.

The ship settled onto the ground.

The Waiting

For several moments nothing happened.

The crowd stood quietly at a respectful distance.

Even the wind seemed to pause.

Torlan stood beside **Dr. Arel Ziv**, his eyes fixed on the unfamiliar vessel.

Up close, the ship looked smaller than the massive colony vessel whose wreckage still lay scattered across the distant hills. But its design was unmistakably human—smooth metal surfaces, careful engineering, and symbols painted along the side of the hull.

Ziv spoke softly beside him.

"Your people have come a long way."

Torlan nodded.

"Yes."

He could feel his heartbeat quickening.

For most of his life, humanity had existed only in the pages of the ship logs.

Now they stood only a few dozen steps away.

The Door Opens

A hatch along the side of the spacecraft slowly lowered.

A ramp extended toward the ground with a soft mechanical hum.

Several figures appeared in the opening.

They wore protective suits designed for alien environments. Their helmets reflected the bright morning sunlight, hiding their faces behind mirrored visors.

The figures stepped down the ramp cautiously.

Their movements were careful as they adjusted to the powerful gravity of Cyrion.

One of them paused halfway down the ramp and looked toward the gathering of Cyrion citizens.

Then the figure reached up and removed their helmet.

The First Human Face

A woman stood at the base of the ramp.

Her hair moved slightly in the morning wind.

Her eyes scanned the valley with open amazement.

For the first time in his life, Torlan was looking at someone who looked like him.

Human.

The realization struck him with unexpected force.

The shape of her face.

The color of her skin.

The familiar structure of her eyes.

All of it reflected something he had never fully understood until this moment.

The woman noticed him standing near the front of the crowd.

Her gaze lingered.

Then she stepped forward.

The Introduction

The woman spoke slowly, choosing her words carefully.

"Greetings," she said.

"My name is **Commander Elena Vance** of the exploration vessel *Aurora Pathfinder.*"

Her voice carried across the quiet field.

"We have come searching for the colony ship *Horizon Dawn*, which disappeared twenty years ago."

A murmur moved through the gathered townspeople.

Vance continued.

"Our records indicate the vessel may have crashed somewhere on this planet."

She paused, scanning the faces before her.

"Did anyone here find such a wreck?"

The Answer

Dr. Arel Ziv stepped forward calmly.

"Yes," he said.

The commander's expression sharpened immediately.

"You located the wreck?"

"Yes."

"And the passengers?"

Ziv hesitated for only a moment.

Then he answered.

"Most did not survive."

The commander's face fell slightly.

"That is what we feared."

The Survivor

Ziv placed a hand gently on Torlan's shoulder.

"But one did."

Commander Vance looked toward the young man standing beside him.

Her eyes widened.

"You're… human."

Torlan nodded.

"Yes."

The commander studied him carefully, disbelief slowly turning into wonder.

"You survived the crash?"

"I was a child."

"And you lived here?"

Torlan looked across the valley.

"Yes."

Two Worlds Meet

For a moment the field remained completely silent.

The Cyrion citizens watched the visitors with quiet curiosity.

The humans from the ship studied the valley and its people with equal fascination.

Commander Vance finally spoke again.

"We never expected to find anyone alive."

Torlan smiled faintly.

"Neither did I."

Ziv's Pride

Ziv looked at the young man beside him.

"He has grown strong here."

The commander nodded.

"That is clear."

She glanced toward the towering cliffs and heavy skies surrounding the valley.

"Surviving on a world like this would not be easy."

Ziv smiled quietly.

"No."

Then he added,

"But he did more than survive."

Closing Image

Later that afternoon the visitors from Earth walked through the streets of Valaryn, guided by Ziv and Torlan.

Children stared in amazement at the strange clothing and equipment of the newcomers.

The humans stared just as openly at the towering stone buildings and powerful Cyrion citizens.

Two worlds were meeting for the first time.

And at the center of that meeting walked a young man who belonged to both.

Chapter 20 — The Choice of Torlan

The spacecraft remained in the valley for three days.

During that time the visitors from Earth carefully examined the wreckage of the *Horizon Dawn.* Their instruments scanned the scattered debris fields beyond the western ridges, confirming what Torlan and the people of Valaryn had long known.

The colony ship had been destroyed beyond repair.

The dream of reaching the distant world called **Hope** had ended on Cyrion.

Yet one part of that journey had survived.

The Invitation

On the third morning **Commander Elena Vance** met with Torlan and **Dr. Arel Ziv** in the garden behind the house.

The blueleaf plants rustled softly in the wind.

Sunlight filtered through the tallroot vines that climbed along the stone walls. The garden carried the quiet warmth of a place that had been tended with care for many years.

Commander Vance studied the garden with quiet appreciation.

"It's beautiful here," she said.

Ziv nodded.

"My wife built it."

Vance looked around again, taking in the peaceful rows of plants and the stone paths that curved gently through the beds.

"She must have loved this place."

"She did," Ziv replied.

After a moment, Vance turned to Torlan.

"We would like you to come with us."

Torlan had known the question would come.

Even so, hearing the words carried unexpected weight.

"Back to Earth?" he asked.

"Yes."

She paused before continuing.

"And if you wish, beyond."

A Larger World

Commander Vance explained what had changed in the years since the *Horizon Dawn* had been lost.

Humanity had expanded across several nearby star systems.

New settlements had been built.

New ships now traveled regularly between worlds.

The universe had grown larger than the colonists aboard the *Horizon Dawn* had ever imagined.

New cities existed beneath alien skies.

New discoveries were being made every year.

"You have a place among us," Vance said gently.

"You always did."

Torlan listened carefully.

The words stirred something deep inside him.

A connection to a world he had never truly known.

The Garden

That evening Torlan sat beside Dr. Ziv on the familiar stone bench in **Lyara's garden**.

The sun was sinking behind the western ridges.

Shadows stretched across the valley as evening slowly settled over Valaryn.

Neither of them spoke for a long time.

Finally Ziv broke the silence.

"You are wondering whether to go."

"Yes."

Ziv nodded slowly.

"That is a very large question."

The Heart of a Choice

Torlan looked across the valley.

The lights of Valaryn were beginning to appear as evening settled over the town.

"This is my home," he said.

"Yes."

"But Earth is where I began."

Ziv folded his hands thoughtfully.

"You belong to both."

Torlan sighed softly.

"That makes the choice harder."

Ziv smiled gently.

"Not necessarily."

Ziv's Wisdom

Ziv gestured toward the garden around them.

"When Lyara planted these gardens, she used seeds from many different regions of Cyrion."

Torlan looked at the plants surrounding them.

Each one had its own shape and color.

Some grew tall.

Others spread low along the soil.

Yet together they formed a single living landscape.

"They all grow here," Ziv continued.

"Even though they began somewhere else."

Torlan understood the meaning immediately.

"You think I should go."

Ziv shook his head.

"I think you should follow the path that allows you to do the most good."

The Goodbye

The next morning the people of Valaryn gathered near the landing field.

The spacecraft's engines were already warming.

A faint vibration hummed through the ground as the vessel prepared for departure.

Commander Vance stood near the ramp, waiting.

Torlan walked slowly toward the ship.

Beside him stood Dr. Arel Ziv.

Neither spoke for several steps.

Finally Ziv said quietly,

"You came to Cyrion as a child who could barely stand."

Torlan smiled slightly.

"That seems like a long time ago."

Ziv nodded.

"You have become something rare."

Torlan looked at him.

"What is that?"

Ziv's eyes were warm.

"A good man."

A Final Lesson

Torlan paused at the base of the ramp.

"What if I make mistakes out there?" he asked.

Ziv smiled.

"You will."

Torlan laughed softly.

"That does not sound very encouraging."

Ziv placed a hand on his shoulder.

"The important thing is that you will continue learning."

Ruun

Beside the ramp **Ruun** waited.

The Varik had followed Torlan all the way to the landing field.

Torlan knelt and wrapped his arms around the animal's thick neck.

"You stay here," he said quietly.

Ruun pressed his head against Torlan's shoulder.

The creature understood more than most animals.

But this journey was not meant for him.

After a moment Torlan stood again.

The Departure

Torlan climbed the ramp.

At the top he turned and looked back.

The valley of Valaryn stretched beneath the bright morning sky.

The **Stone Forest** rose along the distant ridges.

The **Lumar Plains** glowed faintly in the far distance.

And near the garden gate stood the man who had raised him.

Dr. Arel Ziv lifted a hand in farewell.

The Future

The ramp closed.

Moments later the engines ignited.

The spacecraft lifted slowly from the field.

From the window Torlan watched Cyrion grow smaller beneath him.

The world that had shaped his life was fading into the distance.

But it was not leaving him.

Everything he had learned there would travel with him.

Closing Image

High above the planet, the ship turned toward the stars.

Torlan looked once more at the glowing curve of Cyrion below.

He had come to that world as a lost child.

He was leaving it as something else entirely.

A man who had learned strength.

Endurance.

And compassion.

And somewhere ahead, among the distant stars, another world was waiting to meet him.

Epilogue — The Man from Cyrion

Several weeks later, the exploration vessel *Aurora Pathfinder* entered orbit around Earth.

From the observation window, Torlan watched the planet slowly rotate beneath the ship.

Blue oceans.

White cloud systems.

Vast continents stretching across the surface.

He had seen images of Earth many times in the logs of the *Horizon Dawn*, but seeing the world with his own eyes felt very different.

This was the place where his story had begun.

Yet it did not feel entirely like home.

Commander Elena Vance stepped beside him.

"It's beautiful, isn't it?" she said.

Torlan nodded.

"Yes."

For a moment they stood quietly together.

Ships moved slowly through the orbital lanes around the planet, their lights glinting in the sunlight. Stations floated high above the atmosphere, connecting the growing network of human settlements scattered across nearby star systems.

Humanity had grown far beyond the small colony mission that had once carried the *Horizon Dawn.*

Vance glanced toward him.

"You're unusually calm for someone seeing Earth for the first time."

Torlan smiled slightly.

"I suppose I've had time to think about it."

She nodded.

"That tends to help."

A Different Kind of Strength

Later that day Torlan stepped onto Earth for the first time.

The gravity felt light.

Almost strangely light.

Each step required less effort than he expected.

For most people, the weight of Earth was simply normal.

But after years on Cyrion, the difference was unmistakable.

He moved easily through the corridors of the orbital station.

Too easily.

Commander Vance noticed.

"You're adjusting quickly."

Torlan shrugged.

"I spent my childhood on a very heavy world."

Vance smiled.

"That must have been quite an education."

"It was."

The Questions

News of the survivor from the *Horizon Dawn* spread quickly.

Scientists asked questions about Cyrion.

Explorers asked about its gravity and storms.

Engineers studied the records from the wreckage.

But the questions Torlan heard most often were simpler.

"What was it like growing up there?"

Torlan usually answered the same way.

"It was difficult."

He would pause.

"But it was also good."

A Memory of Valaryn

Sometimes, late at night, Torlan found himself thinking about the valley of Valaryn.

The stone paths.

The quiet library.

The wind moving through the Stone Forest.

And the small garden where Dr. Arel Ziv had taught him patience.

He remembered the glowing light of the Lumar Plains.

The sound of the Storm Walls rolling across the valley.

And the steady wisdom of the man who had raised him.

Where you begin does not decide who you become.

Those words remained with him.

The Future

Months later, Torlan stood inside a training facility on one of Earth's orbital stations.

Around him young explorers prepared for their first missions beyond the solar system.

New ships were being built.

New worlds were being charted.

Humanity was still expanding.

Still learning.

Still searching.

One of the instructors approached him.

"We're assembling a new survey crew," the instructor said.

Torlan looked up.

"For where?"

"A heavy world in the Tau Ceti system."

The instructor studied him with a slight smile.

"We thought you might be interested."

Torlan returned the smile.

"Yes."

"I believe I would."

Final Image

Far away, beneath the heavy skies of Cyrion, the valley of Valaryn continued its quiet life.

The wind moved through the Stone Forest.

The Lumar Plains glowed softly each night.

And in Lyara's garden, Dr. Arel Ziv sometimes looked up at the stars.

He knew that somewhere among those distant lights traveled the boy he had raised.

No longer the fragile child who had fallen from the sky.

But a man strong enough to walk between worlds.

A man who carried Cyrion with him wherever he went.

Author's Note
The Worlds That Shape Us

Stories about distant planets often focus on technology, starships, and strange new landscapes. Those things are certainly part of the wonder of science fiction. But at its heart, this story is about something simpler.

It is about the places that shape us.

Every person grows up somewhere. Sometimes that place is the town where we were born. Sometimes it is the community that welcomed us when we arrived as strangers. Sometimes it is simply the group of people who chose to care for us when life did not go as planned.

For Torlan, that place was the valley of Valaryn.

He arrived on Cyrion as a fragile child who could barely stand beneath the planet's heavy gravity. Yet over time the people of that world taught him patience, endurance, and compassion. They showed him that strength is not simply the ability to overcome difficulty, but the willingness to help others endure it.

In many ways, Torlan's journey reflects something that is true for all of us.

Our beginnings matter, but they do not determine who we become.

The people who guide us, the challenges we face, and the communities that welcome us all play a role in shaping our lives. Sometimes we carry pieces of several worlds within us—the place where we began and the place where we truly learned how to live.

Science fiction gives us the freedom to imagine distant stars and new civilizations. Yet the most meaningful stories often remind us that no matter how far we travel, the lessons we carry with us come from the people who helped raise us along the way.

Where we begin is only part of the story.

The rest is written by the worlds—and the people—that help us grow.

— *Russell McFall*

Appendix I — The People of Valaryn

A Character Guide for **Raised Among Giants**

The following individuals represent the most important residents of the valley town of **Valaryn**, the place where the child Bill Arden grows into the man known as **Torlan Tarsen**.

Dr. Arel Ziv
Role: Scientist, physician, mentor, and father figure
Age: Approximately 95 (middle-aged by Cyrion standards)
A respected medical scientist who chose the quiet town of Valaryn over the larger cities of Cyrion. After the crash of the *Horizon Dawn*, he discovers the surviving human child and chooses to raise him. Through patience, wisdom, and quiet example, Ziv becomes the guiding influence in Torlan's life.

Lyara Ziv
Role: Late wife of Arel Ziv
Presence: Remembered through the garden and stories
Lyara created the beautiful garden behind the Ziv home, a place that becomes emotionally important throughout Torlan's life. Though she passed away before Bill's arrival, her kindness and spirit remain present through Arel's memories.

Tarin Sol
Role: Librarian of Valaryn
A patient teacher and devoted scholar. Tarin introduces Bill to the **Library of Valaryn** and encourages his growing curiosity about knowledge and history. She is one of the first to recognize his unusual mind.

Ruun the Varik

Role: Torlan's loyal companion

A powerful predator native to Cyrion, roughly the size of a large Earth wolf but far stronger due to the planet's heavy gravity. After Bill helps the injured animal as a child, Ruun forms a lifelong bond with him and remains at his side through adolescence.

Lina Vareth

Role: Child rescued by Torlan

An energetic and adventurous girl whose curiosity leads her to climb the valley cliffs. When she becomes trapped on a ledge, Torlan rescues her — the first time the town witnesses his courage.

Dalen Kor

Role: Builder and engineer of Valaryn

A practical and good-humored craftsman who often works alongside Torlan during his teenage years. Dalen teaches him the importance of skilled labor and careful construction.

Mira Solan

Role: Keeper of the Learning Hall

Responsible for early education and the **Trials of Youth** in Valaryn. Mira recognizes that Bill learns differently from Cyrion children but encourages his perseverance.

Jarek Thorne

Role: Leader of Stormwatch

A serious and experienced citizen responsible for monitoring the powerful **Storm Walls** that cross Cyrion's plains. During the great storm, he works alongside Torlan to organize the town's defenses.

Elder Vareth

Role: Member of the Valaryn Council

A thoughtful and observant elder who represents the town's leadership. He plays a key role in recognizing Bill's contributions and supporting the decision to give him the name **Torlan Tarsen**.

Kelan Tor

Role: Farmer of the valley fields

A hardworking and friendly farmer who offers Bill small jobs as he grows older. Kelan often remarks on the young boy's determination despite his physical challenges.

Sera Vion

Role: Market keeper

A cheerful and talkative merchant who provides Bill part-time work during his teenage years. Sera becomes one of the townspeople who openly admires Torlan Tarsen's character.

The Children of Valaryn

Bill's early companions during childhood games and schooling. Their interactions reveal his early struggles to adapt to Cyrion's gravity and culture, as well as the gradual acceptance he earns through perseverance.

Characters Beyond Valaryn

Lord William Arden

Role: Torlan's grandfather

A dignified and determined leader who never stops searching for the lost colony ship *Horizon Dawn.* His persistence eventually leads to the expedition that discovers Torlan Tarsen on Cyrion.

Commander Elena Vance

Role: Captain of the exploration vessel *Aurora Pathfinder*

An experienced and disciplined explorer who leads the mission that finally arrives at Cyrion and discovers the survivor of the *Horizon Dawn.*

Community Groups

The Valaryn Council

A small group of elders responsible for guiding the town's decisions and preserving its traditions.

Stormwatch Team

Citizens who monitor the planet's powerful weather systems and warn the valley when Storm Walls approach.

Library Scholars

Researchers and archivists who preserve the accumulated knowledge and history of Cyrion.

Appendix II — Selected Words of the Cyrion Language

From the world of **Raised Among Giants**

The language spoken in the valley of **Valaryn** contains many ancient words that reflect the values and environment of the people of Cyrion.

Torlan Tarsen
Torlan — Enduring traveler / one who walks the long path
Tarsen — son of strength / bearer of strength
A title given to someone who continues forward despite hardship and grows strong among those greater in strength.

Varik
A powerful hunting creature native to Cyrion.
Known for loyalty, intelligence, and deep bonds with trusted companions.

Valaryn
The valley town where Torlan Tarsen is raised.
The name is often translated as *"the valley of learning and endurance."*

Velara
A term of deep affection meaning *beloved companion* or *trusted partner in life*.

Solari
A traditional greeting meaning *peace be with you.*
Often spoken when meeting someone at the beginning of the day.

Tarin

Teacher, librarian, or keeper of knowledge.

A title given to those responsible for preserving learning and history.

Lumar

The glowing moss plains that stretch beyond the valley.

At night the land shines faintly with natural bioluminescence.

Vareth

The towering stone formations known as the *Stone Forest.*

The word is often associated with strength, endurance, and age.

Kyren

The distant guiding star often used for navigation across the plains.

Additional Cultural Words

These terms appear in stories and traditions of Valaryn.

Stormwall

The immense weather fronts that sweep across Cyrion's plains, bringing powerful winds and lightning.

Stonepath

A common name for the carved walking paths that wind through the valley cliffs.

Sky River

The bright band of stars visible across the night sky.

First Standing

A traditional moment in childhood when a young person successfully adapts to Cyrion's heavy gravity.

Endurance Name

A title given by the elders to someone who has proven strength of character through actions rather than words.

Appendix III — World Guide to Cyrion

A Brief Planetary Overview

The planet **Cyrion** is a powerful world of towering landscapes, heavy gravity, and resilient life. Though difficult for humans to inhabit, it has supported thriving civilizations for many generations.

Gravity
Cyrion's gravity is significantly stronger than Earth's. Visitors from lighter worlds often struggle to stand or move for extended periods. Native life has evolved dense muscle structures and strong skeletal systems to adapt to the planet's weight.
For this reason, even simple tasks can become great trials for newcomers.

Weather
The planet is known for immense storm systems called **Storm Walls**. These massive atmospheric fronts move across the plains with powerful winds, lightning, and heavy rain. Settlements such as Valaryn build wind barriers and shelters to withstand their passage.

Landscapes
Cyrion's terrain includes a variety of dramatic environments.

The Stone Forest
Towering rock formations carved by centuries of wind and erosion. The formations create narrow valleys and sheltered paths.

The Lumar Plains
Vast fields of glowing moss that illuminate the night with soft natural light.

The High Ridges
Rocky elevations surrounding Valaryn that provide natural protection from storms.

Wildlife
Life on Cyrion is adapted to the planet's demanding conditions.

Varik
Large hunting creatures known for intelligence, loyalty, and strong bonds with trusted companions.
Other native species include small cliff-climbing animals and high-flying night birds that glide through the dense atmosphere.

The Valley of Valaryn
The town of **Valaryn** lies within a sheltered valley between the Stone Forest and the Lumar Plains.
The settlement is known for:

- learning and scholarship
- careful stewardship of the land
- strong community cooperation

Here, a lost child from another world was raised among the people of Cyrion.
In Valaryn he learned the lessons that would shape his life.
Strength.
Endurance.
And compassion.

Appendix IV — A Short Timeline of the *Horizon Dawn*

The colony vessel *Horizon Dawn* was launched as part of humanity's early interstellar expansion program. Its mission was to establish a new settlement on the distant world known as **Hope**.

The events that followed would change the life of one child—and eventually connect two worlds.

Year 0 — Launch

The colony ship *Horizon Dawn* departs Earth carrying scientists, engineers, and families bound for the settlement world Hope.

Among the passengers are **Elena Arden** and her infant son, **William Arden II**.

Year 1 — Catastrophic Failure

During the journey, the vessel experiences a critical navigation and propulsion failure while passing through an unexplored region of space.

The ship loses control and is pulled off course.

Year 1 — Crash on Cyrion

The *Horizon Dawn* enters the atmosphere of the heavy-gravity planet **Cyrion** and crashes beyond the western ridges near the valley of Valaryn.

Most passengers perish in the disaster.

One child survives.

Year 1 — The Discovery

Dr. **Arel Ziv**, a scientist living in the valley town of Valaryn, discovers the surviving infant among the wreckage.
He brings the child home and chooses to raise him as his own.
The boy is given the name **Bill**.

Years 2–15 — Life in Valaryn

Bill grows up under Cyrion's crushing gravity.
With patience, training, and the support of the community, he slowly becomes strong enough to live and work among the people of the valley.
During these years he forms friendships, learns the ways of Cyrion, and earns the respect of the town.

Year 16 — The Name

After acts of courage and endurance, the elders of Valaryn give Bill a Cyrion name.
Torlan — Enduring traveler / one who walks the long path
Tarsen — son of strength / bearer of strength

Year 20 — The Search Continues

Far from Cyrion, **Lord William Arden** continues his long search for the missing colony vessel.
His persistence eventually leads to a new expedition.

Year 20 — Arrival of the *Aurora Pathfinder*

Commander **Elena Vance** arrives at Cyrion aboard the exploration ship *Aurora Pathfinder*.
The wreck of the *Horizon Dawn* is confirmed.

To the surprise of the mission crew, one passenger is still alive.

Year 20 — The Choice

Torlan Tarsen must decide where his future lies.

The world where he was born.

Or the world that raised him.

Year 20 — Departure

Torlan Tarsen leaves Cyrion aboard the *Aurora Pathfinder*, carrying with him the lessons of the valley of Valaryn.

Strength.

Endurance.

Compassion.

Appendix V — Ships of the Story

The Horizon Dawn and *The Aurora Pathfinder*

Two spacecraft play important roles in the story of Torlan Tarsen. Though built in different eras of human exploration, both vessels represent humanity's enduring desire to reach new worlds.

CSV *Horizon Dawn*

Type: Interstellar Colony Vessel

Mission: Transport settlers to the colony world *Hope*

The *Horizon Dawn* was one of the early long-range colony ships launched during humanity's first expansion beyond Earth. Designed to carry families, scientists, engineers, and agricultural specialists, the vessel was built for long-duration travel across interstellar distances. The ship contained living quarters, agricultural modules, education facilities, and large storage sections intended to support the creation of a new settlement once the colonists arrived.

During its journey, the *Horizon Dawn* suffered a catastrophic failure that forced it off course. The ship eventually crashed on the heavy-gravity world of **Cyrion**, ending the original mission.

Most of the passengers were lost in the disaster.

One child survived.

That child would grow up to become **Torlan Tarsen of Valaryn.**

EV *Aurora Pathfinder*

Type: Exploration and Recovery Vessel

Captain: Commander Elena Vance

The *Aurora Pathfinder* represents a newer generation of human spacecraft built during a later era of interstellar exploration.

Unlike the large colony vessels, the *Pathfinder* is smaller, faster, and equipped with advanced scanning instruments designed to locate lost missions, chart unknown systems, and support long-range reconnaissance.

The ship was dispatched after years of investigation into the disappearance of the *Horizon Dawn.* Following a long search through several star systems, its instruments detected debris consistent with the lost colony vessel on the world of Cyrion.

When the *Aurora Pathfinder* landed in the valley near Valaryn, its crew expected only to confirm the wreck.

Instead, they discovered something extraordinary.

A survivor.

A Bridge Between Two Worlds

The crash of the *Horizon Dawn* brought a human child to Cyrion.

The arrival of the *Aurora Pathfinder* opened the path back to the stars.

Between those two ships stands the life of **Torlan Tarsen**, a man shaped by two worlds.

Appendix VI — A Map of the Valley of Valaryn

A Map of the Valley of Valaryn

The valley of **Valaryn** rests between the western ridges of Cyrion and the distant glow of the **Lumar Plains**. Sheltered by high stone formations and protected by ancient wind barriers, the town grew slowly around its gardens, learning halls, and irrigation channels. Many of the events of Torlan Tarsen's early life occurred within this quiet valley.

Above is a simplified map showing the most important locations.

Key Locations

Valaryn Town

The small valley settlement where Torlan Tarsen grows up. It contains the Library, the Learning Hall, the Market Hall, and the homes of the townspeople.

Lyara's Garden

The garden behind the home of Dr. Arel Ziv. It becomes one of the most important emotional places in Torlan Tarsen's life.

Northern Wind Barriers

Ancient structures that redirect the powerful Storm Walls that sweep across Cyrion.

The Stone Forest

Massive natural pillars of rock carved by centuries of wind. Torlan Tarsen learns to climb here as he grows stronger.

The Lumar Plains

A vast field of glowing moss that illuminates the landscape at night with soft blue light.

The Ridge Trail

The high path overlooking the valley where Torlan Tarsen spends his night alone and reflects on his place between two worlds.

A Quiet Place in a Larger Universe

Though the valley of Valaryn is small, it becomes the place where Torlan Tarsen learns strength, endurance, and compassion.
From this quiet valley, his journey eventually leads back to the stars.

About the Author

Russell McFall is a lifelong storyteller who enjoys exploring the human side of science fiction. His stories focus on character, courage, and the quiet choices that shape a person's life.

Before becoming a full-time writer, Russell spent many years working in **software development**, where logic and problem-solving were part of everyday life. At the same time, he and his wife devoted many years to **children's ministry and homeschooling their family**, experiences that deeply influenced the themes found in his writing.

Many of Russell's stories first began as **bedtime adventures told to his children**. Those early stories gradually grew into larger worlds filled with explorers, young heroes, and distant planets where character matters as much as technology.

Russell enjoys writing **clean, thoughtful science fiction** that can be read and enjoyed by both younger readers and adults. His books often explore themes of perseverance, responsibility, friendship, and the quiet strength that grows through adversity.

He continues to write and develop new stories in his **Space Cadet series and other science-fiction adventures**, always with the goal of creating stories that inspire imagination while encouraging courage and integrity.

Russell lives in the United States and continues writing with the same sense of wonder that first inspired those early bedtime stories many years ago.

Also by Russell McFall

Ordained Path Books

Clean Science Fiction and Inspirational Writing for Thoughtful Readers

---

Contemporary Fiction and Short Stories

Stories of Community, Memory, and Hope

- **Squirrel Creek Estates — Where the Porch Lights Stay On**
- **The World That Chose**

The Space Cadet Richard Series

Where the Legacy Began

- **The Final Countdown**
- **The Dunes of Dinkytown**
- **The Mastermind's Maze**

The Space Cadet Legacy Series

Over 30+ novels of courage, friendship, and discovery — including

- **The First Gate**
- **Welcome Back, Player**
- **Flibber's Journey Home**
- **Stronger Together**
- **Phasegate Rising**
- **The Makers' Handshake**
- **Optimized**

(New missions continuing.)

Literary Humor and Reflections

Serious Nonsense — Sanity Sold Separately

Devotional and Reflection Books

- **Remembering God's Help — Stone by Stone**
- **Attributes of God**
- **This Is My Story, This Is My Song**
- **Lives of Faith**
- **Foundations of Faith**

Russell McFall writes clean fiction and thoughtful reflections designed to uplift the heart, sharpen the mind, and remind every reader that light still wins.

www.ingramcontent.com/pod-product-compliance
Lightning Source LLC
LaVergne TN
LVHW010659110826
845149LV00014B/3167
9781972724002